SONG OF THE SAGANI

LAST SWORD IN THE WEST
BOOK 6

RYAN KIRK

WATERSTONE
MEDIA

For Chris

1

———

Quinton stepped through the door of the mission and was awed by the size of the interior. The walls shot halfway to the sky before the supporting pillars arched to form the steeply angled roof. Enormous stained-glass windows cast a colored mosaic of light across the pews and the gathered worshippers. The enormity of the mission engendered the same sense of smallness he experienced riding across the open plains.

He'd spoken with the men and women who designed the mission, and they'd been pleased to hear his impressions. Darla, who headed the team, had told him the mission was more than a mere building. He still remembered her words, as he'd meditated on them often since.

"It reminds us of the glory of the Creator," she'd said, her eyes filled with wonder as she gazed upon the recently completed marvel. "When anyone, believer or not, steps within these walls, they'll *feel* the majesty of the Creator. They won't need convincing because they'll know the truth deep in their bones."

Darla's faith struck a chord that resonated still. She had created a structure that would last long after she returned to the Creator's loving embrace. Some nights, when Quinton doubted the paths he'd chosen, he wondered if the Creator would view his own labors as kindly as Darla's.

He couldn't guess the Creator's mind. In his years of service, he'd done more to spread the word than almost anyone alive, but he'd committed a terrible sin to accomplish his ends. He'd welcomed a demon into his holy flesh.

Quinton reached the first rug laid a few paces within the entryway. He dropped to his knees with the ease of water flowing downstream, then bowed until his forehead touched the floor. The cool tile calmed his racing thoughts.

He was already damned to the three hells. His fate had been decided the day he elected to host a demon to better serve the Creator. Though he didn't know the Creator's thoughts, the Holy Father spoke with the Creator's voice, and he blessed Quinton's endeavors.

So his questions were pointless. He could fret about whose contribution stood larger, but such thoughts were nothing but evidence of his human frailty. They all served the Creator with the gifts given to them. He knew as much, but a shadow of doubt lingered in his heart.

He rose to his feet, took three steps forward, then repeated the process on a second rug. A third repetition on a final rug granted him entrance to the sanctuary. Three humblings to remind him of his place and the glory of the Creator. Three times he pressed his forehead to the stone to remember the three hells that awaited unbelievers and the fallen.

The ritual centered him. Extraneous worries dropped away, allowing his focus to settle on the Creator. He slid into an empty pew and bowed his head. The priest spoke of redemption and of the great trials that the faithful would endure on their path to salvation. Quinton took comfort in the message, as he often did.

A knight sat beside him near the end of the service. She bowed her head and whispered the words of sending as the priest blessed the congregation.

The priest bowed deeply to those gathered, and they stood and bowed in return. A group of church elders then stepped forward from the frontmost pews and turned to conduct the day's work. The knight leaned over to whisper in Quinton's ear, but he held up a finger to delay her. He wanted to use his sharp hearing to listen to the conversations between the elders and the congregation.

One petitioner came looking for work. He had kept ledgers for a business back east, but when they'd learned of his faith, they'd thrown him to the street. The elder promised a well-paying position within the week, then asked if the man needed any money until then. The bookkeeper shook his head. They arranged a future meeting to discuss the details, and the petitioner left the sanctuary with his back straight and a light in his eye.

An older woman asked for medicine for her sick son, and two young men who looked like brothers sought permission to join the church's army. Quinton watched and listened to every exchange, enraptured.

The knight's patience quickly wore thin. "What do you find interesting here? This is no more and no less than what happens in every mission across the country."

"It's no less inspiring for being common. Whoever doubts the Creator cares for his creation has to look no farther than the nearest mission. I once served in the government's army, which had every reason to treat its soldiers well, yet it didn't come close to the care these elders provide the most helpless of petitioners."

The knight almost rolled her eyes, then looked at him and remembered whom she was talking to. "Of course, sir."

Quinton didn't chastise her. Her mind was on other matters, so it was understandable that she might sometimes forget the reason they fought. "Is he here?" he asked.

"He's waiting for you downstairs."

Quinton followed her lead back toward the entryway. She turned before the rugs and led him to a recessed door guarded by two more knights. She opened the door, revealing a set of stairs leading beneath the sanctuary. The knights closed the door behind them.

The stairs ended in a long hallway. His escort stopped at the third door on the right and knocked softly. The door opened into a richly appointed office, with two more knights standing guard within.

Quinton fell to his knees and bowed his head at the sight of the Holy Father. They'd sent messages back and forth, but this was the first time they'd met since Quinton's failure. "Father, forgive me."

Father didn't respond, but Quinton heard the soft sound of cloth rustling. The knights in the room marched out and shut the door behind them, leaving Quinton and Father alone. No doubt, Father's guards loathed leaving the Creator's emissary alone with the sinful killer, but Father's wishes couldn't be disobeyed.

"Stand, Quinton. We've known each other too long for such formalities."

Though he didn't feel worthy, he also couldn't disobey a request from Father. "I failed, Father."

"Only in killing Tomas. By all other measures, your efforts were successful."

"If not for Tomas, we might have won Kimson."

"Perhaps. There is no point in worrying about what might have been. At times, the Creator's plan is hidden even from my vision, but such are the times we must rely on faith. No one questions your service."

Quinton couldn't let himself so easily off the hook. "I'm the better sword, and I had him imprisoned. He shouldn't be free."

Father stood and came around the desk. "He shouldn't, but he is. I hear the agony in your voice, old friend. I would forgive you, except there is nothing to forgive. But now I must ask, are you prepared for your next assignment?"

"Is it hunting Tomas?"

"It is far more important, and I fear your perceived loss outside Chesterton blinds you. Are you prepared to serve the church, even if its wishes differ from your own?"

Quinton swallowed his disappointment. He'd ridden back and forth across the prairie these last few months, hunting generals and politicians who stood against the church. His work had mattered, but none of it was what he wanted, which was another chance against the only man who'd crossed swords with him and lived. That Father doubted his commitment after he'd put aside his wishes for so long stung, and Quinton knew Father's question would echo in his thoughts for days.

His answer was so obvious it was almost an insult to have to speak it. His desires meant nothing compared to those of the Creator and his emissary. He bowed. "Of course, Father."

"Good. Tomas interrupted our work at Kimson, but the knowledge we gained there has spread, and one of our greatest minds thinks she has finally discovered the last key to the mystery."

Quinton's eyes, which had been gazing at the floor, shot up. "Truly?"

The excitement on Father's face was answer enough. When he answered, he sounded more like a child in possession of a long-sought secret than a holy man entrusted with the Creator's commands. "Truly. It is not that our time of struggle is at an end. So long as we live in this fallen world, our paths will never be without trouble. But our first tests have proven promising, to the point where I am convinced our theories about the nexuses are correct. In the last test, we took complete control of one. And now this scholar has accomplished another long-held goal."

Father paused, allowing the tension to build. "She killed one!"

The news caused Quinton to step back. He looked to the heavens and offered a quick prayer of thanks to the Creator. "I didn't think I would live to see the day."

"You and me both. Now it looks like our great work may be over in the next year. Two at the most."

"What about the conflict?" Quinton asked.

Father waved away the concern. "It continues, and I expect the army will continue to push us west. We're outnumbered and outgunned. Once we have control of the nexuses, though, it won't matter. Then the army won't be able to advance another step, and all the land we hold that day will be ours forever. You see, don't you, how important this woman is?"

"Everything hinges on her."

"Exactly. Which is why I need you, old friend. She was on her way west when marshals detained her. She's being held in the prison in Razin. Before long, I expect she'll be on a train back east under the protection of an entire army. If that happens, we may lose the war for good. I can't move my own forces without the army responding, but a single man won't raise many eyebrows."

"You want me to get her?"

"Get her and bring her to Corrin. We're building facilities for her there."

"Are there any other concerns?" Quinton asked.

Father shook his head. "The only thing that matters is bringing that scholar west. I don't care what you have to do to accomplish it. As usual, the full resources of the church are at your discretion."

"What forces do we have in Razin?" The town's name was familiar to Quinton, but he couldn't place it. His memory wasn't what it had used to be. He feared it was the first sign of the madness come to take him.

"A mission that barely deserves the name. It was a site of some of our early experiments, but your friend Tomas destroyed them a couple of years ago. That was where he killed the cardinal. Since then, we've not spent much of our effort rebuilding in the area. The town doesn't want us there, and with the research station destroyed, there isn't as much reason for us to obsess over one small town. If there's anything you want or need, best to have it on hand before you get there. Before you leave, I can offer you several suggestions."

Father's reminder unlocked the memories Quinton hadn't been able to find on his own. Yes, he knew Razin. He'd studied the maps and heard the stories of all the people involved there. The church's investigation of the incident had been thorough.

He knew he wouldn't find Tomas there, but while he was in town, there were a few other people he would take the time to visit. People who had helped Tomas stand against the Creator.

Father had told him he could do whatever he wanted, so long as he saved the scholar. He could bring justice and save the church, all in one swing of his blade. He imagined the blood on his sword, and it brought a smile to his lips.

Quinton bowed deep to Father, heart pounding with joy. "I live to serve, Father. It will be done."

2
___

Tomas rested on a small rise that looked out over the camp of General Gavan's 34th Army. Their last battle against the insurgents had ended four days ago, but the evidence of the fight lingered in the camp's mood. A stillness hung in the air as soldiers remembered friends who had passed through the gate before their time. Soft laughter rose from the campfires as soldiers spun tales about the recently departed. Listening to the camp, Tomas felt like fate had seized him by the throat and thrown him deep into his own past. Sure, the horizon was flatter, and the colors of the uniforms were different, but everything else remained the same.

He'd run west as far as his feet could carry him, only to end up in the same place he'd started from.

There had been an instructor at his sword school who claimed that history was a circle, a waltz that danced to the three beats of war, peace, and revolution. Tomas had believed the truth of the claim the first time he heard it, but he'd never expected to live long enough for the circle of history to appear in his own life. Looking down at the camp made him feel old, like the blood in his veins was dust coursing through his body.

He was in a mood, and he knew it. The pointlessness of their battles frustrated him, and he was angry at himself for falling into the same trap he'd first sprung decades ago. When he'd joined the 34th after Kimson, he'd imagined he could do some good, both for himself and for the world.

He'd thought the same after graduating from the sword schools. He'd believed it even more deeply after he'd become a host and grown used to Elzeth's power. Hells, he'd even believed as much when he'd become a criminal, certain that his petty rebellion was more a noble resistance than the foolishness it was.

Every time, the world had taught him its greatest truth: that an individual didn't matter. History moved in currents that no single person could shape. The best most could do was survive. A select few could shape and guide the currents, but never control. He wasn't among them. For all his strength, the best he could do was keep his head barely above water.

He'd fought in several skirmishes over the summer, and he'd spilled as much blood in the past three months as he had in the past five years of wandering. It hadn't made a damn bit of difference. Of course, there were army soldiers alive today that would have died had he not fought, and that was something, but it wasn't anywhere near what he'd hoped to accomplish. He hadn't changed the course of any battle nor proved decisive in any way. All the fresh killing that stained his soul meant nothing.

He'd simply been present.

Elzeth had the good sense to remain silent. They'd both been moody the past few months, and the simplest path to peace was to avoid conversation.

Unfortunately, not everyone recognized the wisdom of the practice. Tomas heard the soldier running from the edge of camp and sighed. He didn't turn to greet her, but his rudeness didn't deter the young woman. She stopped short of him, bowed, and said, "Sir, the general wants to see you."

"I'll be right there."

The woman didn't leave. Tomas turned and shot her a questioning glance. She grimaced. "Sorry, sir, but my instructions are clear. I'm not supposed to leave without you."

Tomas rubbed at his eyes. Gavan knew him too well now. Left alone, Tomas would have waited until much later to report. It wasn't a good time, but there was nothing for it. He stood up and brushed the dirt off his pants. "Fine, lead the way."

The soldier looked relieved, and Tomas idly wondered what she would have done had he refused.

They weaved their way through the camp. Familiar scenes threatened to pull him again into the past, a problem he dealt with more often now. He held out his hands as they walked and stared at them. They were as steady as ever, but that was only a meager relief. By the time the first physical tics appeared, madness was already well on its way to consuming the host. He couldn't guess how much time remained for him.

He didn't fear madness, not exactly. It was as pointless as fearing death. No matter his choices, it was coming for him, so there was little point in worrying about it. No, what he feared was madness stealing him before he'd found some semblance of peace.

The ring of Gavan's honor guard parted at their arrival and closed behind them as soon as they passed. The messenger motioned for Tomas to wait while she stepped into the tent. After a moment of muffled conversation, she emerged and gestured for Tomas to enter. He did and was surprised to find Gavan alone. Most of their meetings took place when the tent was filled to bursting with his commanders. Had he known it was just to be the two of them, he wouldn't have felt the desire to delay the meeting.

"Tea?" Gavan asked, turning to a pot as though the answer was certain. "I just had some water boiled."

Gavan tried to appear nonchalant, but Tomas had studied the general for too long to be fooled. What looked to be casual kindness was a calculated gesture meant to put Tomas at ease. Knowing that put him on edge. "Please."

Gavan indicated Tomas should sit. Tomas chose a small stool and pulled it up to a small table. Gavan sat across from him and prepared the tea. Though the general was getting up in years, his hands were steady and his motions precise. Gavan didn't speak as he worked, and in the silence Tomas imagined the various disasters that might have led to this summoning. Had something happened to Hardin and Ulva?

Gavan finished preparing the tea and presented a cup to Tomas with a generous bow. They took their first sips together. The tea was some of the best Tomas had tasted. Gavan sourced his leaves from some of the finest fields in the mountains out east. The flavor was almost enough to make Tomas consider leadership as a viable future. The income and access to supplies tempted him, though he'd probably not live long enough to fully enjoy the position.

When Gavan finally answered Tomas's unspoken question, he did so directly. "I'd like you to travel southeast to Razin. I understand you're familiar with the town."

Tomas wouldn't have been more surprised if Gavan had announced his retirement and handed command of the 34th straight to him. His expression must have been something because the corner of Gavan's mouth turned up in a smile. It was a sight almost as rare as a wild sagani these days.

"Why?" Tomas asked.

"The marshals there caught a believer traveling through town. She was wanted for three counts of murder, and Army spies believe she's a leading scholar for the church. Her work focuses on the nexuses. They believe she's someone very high up. We'd like you to aid the unit tasked with escorting her east."

There was more that Gavan wasn't saying. Tomas sensed it in the careful way the general chose his words. "Why me, especially if you have a unit already tasked?"

"A few reasons. One is that you're familiar with the machine in Kimson, a line of research the spies tell us this woman was also involved in. You're the only host in the army with any experience of the machine, and we hope you might aid in her interrogation. You'll know questions to ask we might not think of. Also, the 34th is rotating off the front lines for a few months. I didn't think you would want to join another unit, and there's no point in you resting."

Tomas's eyes narrowed. He could think of only one reason Gavan would say something like that. "What have you noticed?"

"Subtle changes. Your attention wanders more than it used to. Your focus isn't as intense as when we first met. No one thing that would cause me to worry, but enough slight changes it's the only explanation that fits. Have you noticed anything?"

Tomas looked at his hands. "Subtle is a good word for it. I've worried but haven't been able to point to any one thing and say, 'This is happening.'"

Gavan blew out a long breath. "I hate to ask it, but any idea how long you have left?"

Tomas shook his head.

If Gavan was disappointed in the answer, his face betrayed nothing. "You want to keep pushing, don't you? That was my assumption."

"I do. If you're taking a few months to rest and recover, it's better I do something with my time, and I'd like to visit Razin again."

"There is one more reason I want you to go. Normally, when we capture someone from the church, there's an entire process that happens behind the scenes. The church demands a release or offers an exchange of their prisoners for ours. Negotiations commence, and eventually, a deal is struck. It's true for their lowest soldiers and their strongest knights. We know this lady is a church agent, but the church has been completely silent about her."

"Ominous," Tomas agreed.

"So you'll do it?"

"Of course."

They spoke of details for a time and then continued conversing until the pot of tea was empty. Gavan and Tomas had crossed paths before the church had turned Tomas's life upside down, and he liked to think there was a mutual respect between them. He suspected Gavan enjoyed talking to him because he wasn't connected to the rest of the army. What they said could be trusted to remain confidential.

When Tomas departed the tent, his heart was heavy. Their goodbyes had a sense of finality, an unspoken assumption that they wouldn't meet again. Tolkin had risen while he'd been inside, and Tomas stared at the moon.

Elzeth stirred, the first movement Tomas had felt from the sagani in weeks.

"Did you know?" Tomas asked.

"Suspected, but like you, wasn't sure," Elzeth said. The

sagani still couldn't read his thoughts, but Tomas's emotions were bright as day to Elzeth, and they'd traveled together long enough that a secret would have been impossible to keep. "And no, I've been searching my memories of the times before, and I don't think I ever stayed with a host long enough for madness to set in."

There were other questions, but Tomas didn't have the courage to ask them. He'd already said his last farewell to one friend tonight. He didn't want to start saying another. "Looks like we're going to Razin."

"Looks like. How do you feel about it?"

It was a bit of a rhetorical question. Elzeth knew perfectly well how he felt, but he also knew that talking about a problem was a way to understand it better.

"Excited, but also scared."

Elzeth said nothing, and Tomas was silent for a moment. Then he admitted the truth.

"Mostly scared."

3

Quinton rode into town and studied the surroundings from atop the horse the church stables had loaned him. This wasn't Razin, but a town four days north called Baldwin. The events at Razin had turned most of the city against the church, leaving the mission there without the resources Quinton would need.

Because the church didn't want to lose precious resources, they had instead funneled all the money, people, and supplies earmarked for the area into the mission in Baldwin. It then fell to Baldwin to support the church's mission throughout the region.

Quinton wanted the knights Baldwin could offer, and Father had been adamant he visit on his way to Razin. He'd hinted at some sort of trouble, but hadn't elaborated. If he was sending Quinton, it was the sort of trouble that needed a sword to solve.

Baldwin wasn't large, even by frontier standards. Quinton guessed the town's population sat somewhere between three and five hundred souls. Passersby greeted him kindly enough, and he tipped his hat in response. As was his practice, he wore no sign of the church upon his person, so he couldn't judge the town's attitude toward the faithful yet. The priest would tell him when they met.

He rented a small room at the local inn. Though the mission would have gladly offered him a bed, it seemed wise to stay mostly out of sight. Marshals watched missions like hawks since the church's battle for independence farther west had begun, and Quinton didn't want to draw any unnecessary attention.

Contacting the mission's priest was a convoluted process. After leaving his saddlebags at the inn and checking to ensure they cared well for his horse, he walked down the street to a shop Father had instructed him to find.

Inside the shop, a large bearded man greeted him, and Quinton gave a quick bow.

"You're new around here," the man said, his voice booming within the small space. "You staying or simply passing through?"

"Just passing through," Quinton said. He pulled a sealed letter from his pocket and handed it to the man. The seal bore the mark of the Holy Father himself.

The man's gaze took in the mark, and his eyes widened. Before he could fire a barrage of questions, Quinton tipped his hat and turned to leave. "If you could get that to the priest before sundown, quietly, I'd be much obliged."

"You bet, sir!" the man said. He sounded like he was about to say more, but Quinton was already stepping out the door.

He spent the afternoon walking Baldwin's streets. If all went well, trouble should be unlikely, but he would be a fool not to prepare for the worst. He studied the structures, mapped out different escape routes, and refined his sense of the people and the place. His study wasn't so much a

conscious effort as a constant process of absorption. He'd
long ago lost track of the number of unknown places he'd
visited in the course of his service, first to the army and now
to the church.

After so many settlements, he'd become numb to the
differences between towns. He was sure that if he bothered,
he would note what distinguished one from the next, but
now all he saw were the similarities to every other place
he'd been. The novelty had worn thin.

After his exploration, he returned to the inn for the
evening meal. He caught a brief bit of sleep after, waking
just as Tolkin rose on the horizon. He slithered out the
window of his room and slid from shadow to shadow across
the streets. No one followed him, but he saw no reason to
abandon the caution that had served him so well over the
years. In time, he reached the mission.

Compared to the missions out west, in the church-
controlled lands, this one was nothing remarkable. The
exterior was well-maintained, a testament both to the
newness of the building and the dedication of its priest.
Otherwise, it was the same design as a hundred other
frontier missions. In the front was a steeple, rising to the
highest elevation in the city. The rest of the building was
rectangular, with a steep roof.

Quinton was less interested in the building than he was
in the man standing outside it. He'd been there earlier in
the day, too, as Quinton had explored the town. When he
moved, Quinton caught the reflection of Tolkin's moonlight
on the marshal's badge.

That might be a problem, but it was why Quinton had
come to the mission first instead of to the meeting place the
note had designated.

Well before their appointed meeting time, a woman in

the robes of a priest emerged from the church. She was shorter than most but stood as tall as any believer should. The priest glared at the marshal, and Quinton decided he liked her. She let the glare linger, then stomped off away from the mission.

The marshal waited for the priest to put some space between them, then followed her. The priest was clearly aware of the tail, but what could she do? She was no warrior, and Father had given all priests and believers strict guidance. Unless they were farther west, fighting to establish their own state, all believers were to renounce violence. The church didn't need more trouble.

Quinton rubbed his chin, then followed the marshal.

Had the lawman been more aware, the process might have been more difficult, but the young man had watched the mission all day and didn't seem concerned about the priest's wanderings. He had the air of a man doing a job, even if he'd rather do almost anything else. He was relaxed, and what focus he possessed was fully on the priest. It was child's play to approach the marshal unobserved.

Quinton knocked the marshal unconscious before he realized the danger. The body fell to the ground, and Quinton saw just how young the marshal was. No wonder he hadn't been focused. He wasn't much older than a kid.

The sound of the body falling caused the priest to turn, and Quinton tipped his hat. He picked up the marshal under the armpits and dragged him to the corner of an alley where it was unlikely a passerby would spot him. The marshal would wake up in a bit, but by then, Quinton would be in the wind, and it would be too late.

The priest bowed far more deeply than was necessary. "You're him, aren't you? The hidden hand of the Holy Father."

Quinton had never heard himself described in those terms, and he was ashamed of the pride that beat in his chest at the title. "I have the honor of serving Father directly, yes."

"We hear rumors about you sometimes. How you appear in the places the faithful need you most. Are you here to help us?"

Quinton almost answered, "No," worried about the complications, but the note of desperation he heard in the priest's voice gave him pause. Father *had* suggested Quinton stop in Baldwin to acquire the knights he sought, and Father rarely did anything without multiple purposes. He answered carefully. "My purposes are my own, but if there is something I can do to aid the faithful in Baldwin, please ask. I can make no promises, but I'll happily do all I can."

The priest sagged with relief. "Ever since the battles out west, the marshals have kept a close eye on us. If it was that alone, their behavior would be nothing but an inconvenience, but in the past few weeks, they've gone even further. Every week a small caravan arrives carrying supplies and pilgrims from the churches out east. Among those supplies is a small shipment of gold coins we use to support our mission. For the last three weeks, the marshals have stopped the caravan. They haven't harmed any of the pilgrims, thank the Creator, but they search until they find the gold."

The priest clenched her fists. "We're on the verge of having to close the mission. We rely on that gold to provide incomes for the faithful. If we don't receive a shipment this week, we won't be able to pay our workers. That's a dozen families who will have to suffer without food."

Quinton's eyes narrowed. "You have knights. It's the reason I'm here. Why not use them?"

"We've decided not to. In part, it's because of Father's injunction. Our welcome in Baldwin hangs by a thread, but the authorities recognize the chaos that would ensue if we were to fall. That's not enough to protect us, though, if we start picking fights."

Quinton heard the frustration in her voice and sympathized. Especially out west, the church had become used to unquestioned authority.

She continued, "But the primary reason is because the marshals have a host, and after Razin, the knights don't want to start a fight they aren't sure of winning."

For a few seconds, Quinton dared to hope that Tomas had returned to the area and had been foolish enough to pick up a badge and pin it to his chest. It couldn't be so, though. The priest claimed the marshals had been stealing the gold for weeks, and church spies reported Tomas had been with the 34th just two weeks ago.

"When is the next shipment due to arrive?" Quinton asked.

"In two days."

The decision was simple enough. Quinton's scholar wasn't due to be moved for over a week yet. The marshals wanted ample protection for the prisoner transport and had called for more support. Quinton had traveled fast, so had time to spare. If he could help a dozen faithful families put food on their tables, he'd be glad to do so. If he killed another host in the process, well, so much the better. That was one less demon that would terrify the faithful. Everyone would win.

"I'd be honored to lend a hand. Quickly tell me everything you can, and I'll make sure the next delivery arrives whole and untouched," he said.

4
——————

Tomas scratched at his chin as he looked down at Razin from the small rise he stood on. The town had loomed large in his thoughts since the last time he'd visited. The sight of it stirred up a deep well of emotions, and he couldn't put a name to all of them. He put a lid on that boiling cauldron and ignored it, focusing his attention instead on observing the town.

He wasn't sure "town" was an appropriate description anymore. Razin had nearly doubled in size, yet it still seemed smaller than he thought it should be. Its two main perpendicular thoroughfares were still the heart of the city. The tallest buildings were built there, most of those being two- or three-story shops that allowed the owner to live above. From his vantage point, he could see the familiar wall of Ben's orphanage. When he'd last visited, it had been near the outskirts of the town, and now Razin had swallowed it whole.

He hoped the old man and his children were well. They deserved all the happiness in the world. If not for more important matters, Tomas would have made straight for the old house with the enormous yard. But he told himself that duty came first. And if that duty brought him back to Angela, who was he to complain?

"It's incredible how fast your kind build," Elzeth said. "This world has never seen predators like you before."

The statement was mostly a compliment, but Tomas caught hints of resentment and fear, too.

"We certainly have a way of settling land and making it ours," Tomas admitted.

Elzeth grunted, ending that conversation before it started. Tomas let it slide while he continued to study the bustling city. It was near noon, and the streets were filled. Even from this distance, he could listen to the music of a growing population. The hammering of nails formed the beat, and the sawing of lumber the rhythm. On the west side of town, a group of builders lifted a wall into position. Farther to the east, he heard the clanging of a hundred men building the railroad into town. They only had a few miles to go before their work was complete and trains could travel here. Razin's growth to this point would be a pittance compared to what was soon coming.

Razin wouldn't be the westernmost town with a railroad. That honor went to a town about a week south of here called Porum. Tomas was also aware that the church had built a few lines out west connecting their missions, but they didn't travel east, so it was almost as though they didn't count.

Porum wasn't growing like Razin, and the competing railroad that had built the line was regretting their investment more with every passing day. Porum was where Tomas was supposed to escort the scholar to, though. Once they got her on the train, not even the church could catch her.

"You're delaying," Elzeth said.

Tomas didn't respond.

Elzeth sighed. "You humans are too complicated. Waiting isn't going to change anything, so you might as well get moving."

True as the advice was, it didn't motivate Tomas forward. He'd thought about Angela the entire way down here, and he still didn't have the slightest clue how this meeting would go. He wasn't even sure if she still lived and worked here. Little news about Razin had reached him while he was out west with the 34th.

Eventually, the growing heat of the afternoon sun pushed him forward. The only real shade for miles was in the town, and the day's warmth made the tree-lined thoroughfares even more inviting.

Unlike before, his arrival didn't garner any special attention. The town had gotten too big to care about every new arrival. It was a simple matter to become one of the faceless masses. He found a new inn, off the major thoroughfares, where he wouldn't be recognized, paid for a room, and stabled his horse. Once that was done, he took a quick bath. Elzeth grumbled about his delay, but it wasn't like they were in a rush.

When he was clean and shaved, he left the inn for the marshal's office.

The walk unsettled him. Much of what he passed was familiar, but there was so much new construction it still felt as though he was visiting Razin for the first time. The juxtaposition of the recognizable and the different left him feeling a little lost. Before long, he stood in front of the marshal's office. Like the city, it had grown in his absence. The blocky building was twice the size he remembered, and he stood on the other side of the street while working up his courage to enter.

"We're going to go mad before you walk through that door," Elzeth complained.

"Just give me a bit, will you?"

Elzeth sighed, but grew silent.

Tomas found a hint of peace in the training exercises he'd been taught to use before battle. He brought his attention to his breath and let his worries slide from his thoughts. Once his mind was almost still, he crossed the street and entered the office.

The first person he saw was Angela, standing outside a cell, talking to a prisoner within. She glanced at the door to check on the new arrival, then froze. Tomas bowed to her. When he straightened, she was halfway to him, and he wasn't sure if she would embrace or punch him.

She did neither. She stopped a few paces away and held herself nearly as still as a statue. "What are you doing here?"

He wished he could discern her emotions the way he did Elzeth's. There was an ocean of feeling hiding beneath the surface of her question, and he couldn't guess at what it held. He feared there were monsters lurking deep within.

A few of the other marshals in the building cast looks their way. Tomas didn't recognize any of them from before, but no one seemed too alarmed to see him. Their looks were the curious glances of strangers and nothing more.

He knew full well that Angela's work meant everything to her, and any familiar displays of affection would be received poorly, so he kept his demeanor professional. He pulled Gavan's orders out of his coat pocket and handed them to her. "I'm here on the orders of General Gavan of the 34th. I'm to assist with a prisoner transport."

She glanced over the papers, and he thought he saw her glaring. "Follow me," she snapped.

"Yes, ma'am."

She spun on a heel and led him quickly through the cells and out the back door of the building. As before, it opened onto a well-maintained training ground. Like the building, the grounds had expanded, but thick walls still surrounded them to keep curious visitors away. Angela slammed the door behind her so they were alone.

"Just what in the three hells do you think you're doing here?" she asked.

"Hi. It's good to see you, too."

She jabbed her index finger at his chest. "You're a wanted man. I should arrest you right here and now."

"I *was* a wanted man." He paused for emphasis. "But General Gavan secured me a pardon." He handed over a second piece of paper. "I keep a copy on me, just in case any overly ambitious marshals think about arresting me."

Angela studied the paper, spending a considerable amount of time on the signature. Her nostrils flared, but then she shook her head and thrust the paper back at him. She was calmer when she spoke again. "Is that real?"

"Every word."

"Even after what happened at Chesterton?"

He wasn't fast enough to mask his reaction, and Angela was too sharp not to notice. He forced himself to meet her gaze, though he feared the judgment she might pass. The weight of his actions in that town still hung like a heavy stone around his neck. "Even after Chesterton."

"Because you're innocent or because the army wants your sword?"

The sliver of hope in her voice was like a knife to his heart. He searched for a way to explain, but anything he would say only sounded like an excuse. He wouldn't stoop so low. "I was not without guilt at Chesterton," he admitted.

She took a step back as though he'd slapped her. "I see."

He stepped toward her. "Angela—"

"No." She held up a hand, and he froze in place.

She looked like a woman fighting a battle with herself, but she was as decisive as ever. "I think it's best if you go now. Where are you staying?"

Tomas gave her the name of the inn.

She nodded. "We're planning on leaving town three mornings from now. That'll put us in Porum a day before the train leaves. If we need something from you before then, I will let you know."

Tomas swallowed hard. He wanted to explain everything, but her expression made her desires clear as crystal. Her hand even inched toward the sword at her hip as though she was prepared for a fight.

Sometimes the best way to win the war was to retreat from a battlefield that was lost. Tomas bowed. "Of course."

He went to the door, opened it, and looked back. Angela stood with her hands on her hips. Tomas searched for some appropriate words, something that would let her know how he felt, but nothing sounded right. He tipped his hat, then left.

She never even wished him farewell.

5

Quinton spent the next two days learning more about Baldwin. Half of winning the battle was understanding the terrain, which only came from spending time on the ground. His first investigations deepened his understanding of the physical topography, but further investigations gave him a deeper sense of the people who lived here. He inquired about work, not because he wanted any, but because understanding what work was available gave him a better sense of how money flowed through town.

What he learned wasn't surprising, but it was helpful. Baldwin, like many frontier towns, was struggling. Dreams pulled settlers west, but reality was much harder to grapple with. Baldwin hadn't won the bid for the railroad station, and it was desperately searching for a reason to continue existing.

The marshals here were well-regarded. Quinton deduced that the marshals were stealing from the church and spreading the money through Baldwin. He heard more than one tale of their incredible generosity.

Noble, Quinton supposed, but foolish. Theft was a sin, no matter how well-intentioned the reasons.

In his investigations, he made excuses to visit the new church arrivals. The priest had told him where to find those who had traveled with the most recent caravans, and Quinton hoped they would share the tale of their assault.

When they learned he was a believer, they welcomed him with open arms and shared their stories. Many were eager to reflect on the trials of the journey, and Quinton loved to listen. He saw the Creator's hand in all their stories. They traveled out west for the same reason he'd become a host, for a new chance at life. It would be up to him to ensure they had the best chance possible.

Even in this, he saw the work of the Creator. He was the only one who could help these families, and the Creator, speaking through Father, had brought him here. He was grateful he could be of service.

As near as he could tell, he didn't raise any suspicions among the townsfolk. The marshals were more focused on the mission, and there were enough travelers coming through that no one paid Quinton much mind.

The night Quinton had met the priest, he'd stolen the marshal's wallet and sword. Rumor in the taverns was that the marshals couldn't decide if the church was planning something or if a marshal had gotten sloppy and been robbed in the very town he was supposed to protect. In response to the attack, the marshals doubled their presence at the mission and patrolled the town in pairs.

Eventually, Quinton reached the last stop on his list. It was a small home, built recently and freshly painted. He knocked on the door. There was a bit of a commotion on the other side, and a few moments later, a pretty young woman answered the door. Her hair was disheveled, and she supported a child on one hip. Quinton heard another child playing in a separate room.

"What?" the woman asked.

"Sorry to bother you, ma'am. Is Jon in?" Quinton asked.

The woman looked him up and down before nodding. She turned back into the house. "Jon, company!"

A thin man with glasses appeared behind the woman and kissed her forehead. She wandered back into the house while the child on her hip stared at Quinton like he was a mystery.

"What can I do for you?" Jon asked.

"My name is Quinton, and I'm a representative of the church. I was wondering if we might speak for a few minutes."

"Of course. Come in, please, and I apologize for the noise and the mess. We're still getting sorted."

"Not a problem at all. I promise I'll be out of your hair soon."

Jon led Quinton through the small house. Crates were piled in one corner of what was supposed to be a bedroom, and the living room had a handful of toys scattered about. Jon's wife was on the floor in the living room, playing with three boys.

The sight was a minor miracle, but it still dimmed the smile on Quinton's face. Once, he'd thought that when his time with the army was done, he'd find the time to fall in love with a woman and build a family together. He dreamed of scenes much like this, and that absence felt like a hole in the pit of his stomach that not even the Creator could fill.

Instead, the Creator had called him down another path. Quinton would always be grateful for the call, but sometimes he wondered what his life might have been. If he'd been allowed to live freely, as others did. Would he be the harried father unpacking crates while his wife taught the children their letters?

His heart ached at the thought, at the paths his life would never take.

But he didn't deserve them, and at least this way, he could help others achieve their dreams.

Jon led him into a small office and closed the door behind them. It didn't shut out the sounds of play completely, but it served well enough. "How can I help?" he asked.

"I'm here about the marshals who ambushed you on your trip into Baldwin, if that's not too much trouble. What can you tell me about the attack?"

Jon related his story quickly. It matched what the other new arrivals had said. The marshals rode in fast, guns drawn. They hit with enough surprise and enough weaponry that it made little sense for the believers to fight back, even though they had weapons of their own. The actual robbery was quite peaceful. Marshals took the gold, left everything else, and rode away.

Jon had been part of the most recent caravan, though, and Quinton was hoping for one important piece of information, a confirmation of a suspicion he'd developed after interviewing other recent arrivals. He asked Jon where the ambush had happened, and Jon described the place, confirming Quinton's suspicions.

The marshals had launched all the recent ambushes from the same location.

They were sloppy, falling into a routine like that, and Quinton would make them pay. He thanked Jon for his time, and at the front door, he pressed a gold coin into the father's hand. Jon's eyes went wide. "I can't take this, sir."

"You can and you will. It's the least I can do to help you

after you've welcomed me into your home. Besides, you have much greater need of it than I."

"I don't know what to say. Thank you."

"You're welcome. Let it serve as a reminder the Creator and his church always look after the faithful."

As he left, he memorized the look of gratitude on Jon's face. It was moments like these that kept him going when doubt assailed his soul.

They reminded him the Creator looked after them all.

The next day, Quinton mounted his horse before the sun rose. He hurried out of Baldwin to seek where the marshals set their ambushes. He found the spot before mid-morning. A small rise in the land protected the ambushers from the view of travelers, but it was easy enough to ride a horse up and down the rise and surprise anyone passing by. It was also close to the road. By the time a caravan understood the danger it was in, it was too late.

The rise was to the west of the road, which traveled almost directly north and south here. Quinton rode up the rise on his horse and down the other side so he could study the ground where he suspected the marshals would wait. Horses and humans had trampled a small area, creating what appeared to be a small campsite.

He looked around. The campsite was at the end of a shallow draw, and another knoll rose to the west of the campsite. Quinton rode up the knoll and looked around. The other side had little to recommend it. He'd hoped for a copse of trees or something that would serve as cover, but the rise dropped and leveled out into featureless plains.

Under most circumstances, he would have searched for a better position, but he suspected the marshals wouldn't even check. It wouldn't occur to them they had become the hunted. His efforts were good enough, so he settled in to wait.

Sometime around noon, he heard more horses approaching. He crawled to the top of the knoll and buried himself in the grass. A group of riders proudly bearing marshal's badges on their chests rode into the small campsite. They dismounted and checked their weapons. One climbed to the top of the rise separating the campsite from the road and hid much the same way Quinton hid from them. Their practiced movements betrayed how routine the ambush had become. None so much as glanced in Quinton's direction.

He counted seven marshals, which had to be near everyone from Baldwin. The town wasn't that large. Five had swords and two carried rifles. But which one was the host that the knights feared?

There. One man was shorter than the others, and his hands trembled. He tried to hide the fact by crossing his arms and stuffing his hands in his armpits, but he fooled no one. The others had the decency to pretend not to notice, though. Fortunately, the host was armed with a sword. Quinton wouldn't have been eager to fight a host with a rifle, though the young man's hands were shaking so badly it might not have mattered.

If there was any concern, it was how close the host was to madness. The descent stole the host's sanity and eventually their life, but in the meantime, it granted them a strength even other hosts were jealous of. The knights had been wise not to attack.

He foresaw no problems, though. Even a host descending into madness wouldn't be fast enough to threaten him. He'd originally planned to charge the group with his horse, but he decided that was an unnecessary risk to the horse. He stayed low in the grass and slithered toward the camp.

The marshals paid no attention to their surroundings. Quinton approached to within a hundred paces before he rose. He commanded the demon within him to burn, and it lit on fire like dry kindling. As always, he reveled in the power the demon granted him. Though the price was his soul, there were days when the sacrifice seemed very much worth it. Quinton sprinted forward as the marshals reacted too slowly to the stranger in their midst.

He went after the two with rifles first. They'd been sitting on the ground beside one another, inspecting their weapons, and Quinton cut them down before they could bring their deadly barrels to bear.

The host caught up to him a moment later.

Quinton leaned back as the host's sword cut about where his head had been. He heard the hiss as the sword passed, and he admired the speed of the cut, even if the results were less impressive. The host stumbled as he tried to turn, and he tripped over his own feet and landed on his bottom. Quinton had seen such problems before. The host wasn't used to the additional speed his descent into madness provided. It was much like a host re-learning how to fight after they absorbed their demon, but with more consistently fatal consequences.

Quinton ignored the host. Despite his speed, he posed little threat with his lack of control. The remaining four marshals tried their best. The host's unintentional distraction had given them enough time to draw their swords and stand, and they shouted at him with unearned bravado. They took comfort in their numbers, which meant next to nothing here. Quinton attacked. Their swords sliced through empty air as he cut them down one at a time.

The battle was over before Quinton felt like he'd gotten started. Only the host remained. Quinton stepped back again as the host missed another cut. Without his speed, this pathetic excuse for a warrior would have been nothing at all. He handled his sword more like a club than sharpened steel. Quinton guessed he'd never been formally trained and that once he became a host, he'd relied on his demon-given strength to protect him.

He was a disgrace to true warriors.

Quinton stabbed him in the throat and smiled as he watched the demon's light fade from the marshal's dying eyes. He'd done the man a favor, but the fight still left him empty inside.

His work protected the church, and it protected families like Jon's, but it didn't satisfy him the way it once had.

Now Tomas, he had been an opponent. Honorable in his own twisted way but skilled with a sword and as brave and foolish as anyone Quinton had ever crossed steel with. Their fights reminded Quinton of what it meant to be alive. They pushed him to be greater than he had been before.

When this was over, he was going to insist he be allowed to hunt Tomas down. He'd ask for the task as a reward, and surely Father would understand.

Killing Tomas was as close to the Creator's blissful afterlife as Quinton would ever get.

He shook himself from his reverie and examined the area. No one lived to tell the tale, and he suspected whatever marshals remained in Baldwin would panic soon enough.

He freed the marshals' horses, rounded up their

weapons to give to the mission, and returned to his own horse. He rode back to Baldwin, confident that for the first time in weeks, the church's caravan would arrive on time and unharmed.

6

Tomas stood outside the marshal's office and looked both left and right. The citizens of Razin went about their daily chores. They bought food, sold nails and tools, and talked to neighbors and friends, oblivious to the way the sky had fallen on Tomas when he wasn't looking. They walked around him as though he was nothing more than a crate or a barrel in their way. None extended him the slightest sympathy.

He'd considered the possibility that Angela wouldn't want to see him. Their parting hadn't been acrimonious, but it hadn't been what either of them wanted. He'd prepared himself to learn that she had found someone else, or that she'd moved to another town, or that she'd moved on in any of a dozen different ways. He'd even wondered if Chesterton would come to haunt him. Every possibility had been examined on his journey here.

But he hadn't really believed in those possibilities. Not deep in his heart. He'd believed that they would speak like old friends, and in time, the flame that had once burned between them would rekindle.

He stared at his palms, searching for any visible tremor. His hands remained steady, but for how much longer?

"She'll come around," Elzeth said.

"What if she doesn't? I had hoped..." He didn't even know how to finish the sentence. What had he hoped for?

Elzeth didn't have the answers, but he tried to shine some sun on Tomas's dark mood. "Don't worry. You'll always have me. At least until I find a better-looking host."

The corner of Tomas's mouth turned up in a smile. "Have to respect the honesty, at least."

He considered visiting Ben now that he had an abundance of free time on his hands, but it was nearing suppertime. They'd be busy feeding the kids and then putting them to bed. Lacking any better options, he returned to the inn. Maybe he'd feel better after a hearty meal and a drink or two.

He passed two new taverns on his way to the inn, and the oblivion they promised tempted him. Both times he slowed, considered, then moved on. Both times he felt Elzeth's relief. "Surprised?" he asked.

"You were quite the mess the last time you parted from her."

Tomas remembered and wished he hadn't. "True enough. Doesn't feel much better this time."

"So what's keeping you sober?"

"If madness is drawing close, I'd rather remember as much as possible, even if it hurts."

Elzeth said nothing, but he didn't have to. Tomas felt the sagani's pride almost as if it was his own.

They reached the inn, and Tomas enjoyed that hearty meal and a glass of wine. The food was better than the army food he'd eaten the last few months, and he lingered longer in the common room than he needed. In one corner, two merchants haggled with a local shop owner over prices. Near the center, a man and woman spoke of tomorrow's travel plans.

It was a pleasant change from the meals with the 34th. Soldiers came from all walks of life, but their service ironed out many of the differences between them. There was a power to that and a camaraderie that would never be found in the common room of an inn, but Tomas appreciated the varied slivers of life he observed. He imagined humanity as a tree, branching in many directions but always reaching upward.

Elzeth's patience wore thin before Tomas's, something more common now than ever. "She's not coming," he said.

Tomas finished the last of his wine. "I know."

When he said it out loud, he almost believed it.

He stood, thanked the innkeeper, and took the stairs to the room two at a time. He stopped at the top and frowned. "You hear that?" he asked.

Elzeth had. "You've got company."

Tomas debated between returning to the common room and barging in on his uninvited guest.

"Might as well introduce yourself," Elzeth said.

Tomas followed the sagani's advice and approached his room. He paused at his door and listened. "Fast or slow?" he asked Elzeth.

Before the sagani could answer, a voice came from the room. "Door's unlocked. Just here to talk, Tomas."

Tomas wasn't inclined to trust a man who broke into another's room while he was away, but there was no surprise to lose. He twisted the handle and opened the door. Elzeth simmered, ready to burst into flames if needed. He poked his head around the open door and saw a man sitting in a chair.

Tomas didn't recognize the visitor. He had a slight build, and his hair was so blonde it almost looked white. It was his eyes that captured Tomas's attention, though. They watched Tomas like a hungry wolf watching a wounded deer limp away. Considering the man knew Tomas's name, it stood to reason he knew Tomas was a host as well, and Tomas couldn't find a trace of concern in his stare.

Tomas closed the door behind him. "You came to talk, so talk. I don't take kindly to uninvited visitors."

The man rolled up one of his sleeves to reveal a tattoo that marked him as one of the Family. Tomas's eyes narrowed, but he kept silent.

"We know why you're here, Tomas. When the time comes to escort that prisoner, you'll get her out of the marshals' grasp and deliver her to me."

Tomas snorted. "And why in the three hells would I do that?"

"Because if you don't, we'll kill Angela, Ben, Olena, and every child who has ever made the mistake of sleeping under Ben's roof."

"Bold choice, threatening children while we're in a room alone together."

The man smiled. "Not so much. My Family has well over a dozen warriors in Razin. If you leave this inn before I do, they go to work."

The man stood. "Now, I've studied you, so I have some idea what you're thinking. You're thinking that maybe you should kill me anyway, then attempt some foolish heroics to stop my Family before they reach everyone."

Tomas had indeed been thinking something along those lines. He was also thinking the man had exaggerated his support. But even if the man only had half a dozen warriors, it was still too many for Tomas to stop in time.

"There's only one problem with your plan." The man took a step toward Tomas. "You can't kill me. You're too slow."

Tomas needed time to think, so he asked the first question that came to mind. "How did you know about me?"

This time, it was the man's turn to snort. "The army is as good at keeping a secret as a sieve is at holding water. Half the country probably knows you're in Razin right now."

"And the prisoner?"

The man shrugged. "The church isn't that much better at keeping secrets."

"Even with the threat, I'm not sure how giving you this researcher is a good idea. I don't want your Family to have a powerful weapon any more than I want the church to have one."

"And you think letting the army control the nexuses is a better idea?"

That question hit close to home. Tomas had been so focused on keeping the prisoner away from the church, he hadn't thought enough about how others might use her similarly. Tomas had respect enough for Gavan and the 34th, but he'd once fought a war against the army, and he wasn't yet convinced he'd made a mistake in doing so.

The man took another step forward. "I'll tell you why you'd want to give us the scholar. The church and the army have something in common. Both of them fear hosts. The church thinks they're a blasphemy against their Creator, but the army's concern is more mundane. To run this country, they need to be the strongest force in the land. It's how you keep law and order. Hosts upset that order."

Tomas thought of Ulva and her little community. "It's

been my experience that most hosts just want to live in peace."

"Sure. But enough want other things. They want power, or freedom, or money. And they have the power to take it. You're living proof. You massacre a third of a town, and a few months later, you're sharing tea with an army general. Most people get hung, and that's if they live long enough to see a trial. Army can't stomach hosts running around any more than the church can. They're just better at not talking about it."

"And your Family will somehow be better?"

"We're the only ones who don't want to see all hosts dead. We want power, freedom, and money, and being a host opens doors to all three. So, you see, we might try to kill you, but it's not because you're a host. It's only because you're in our way."

"I hate that he's making a bit of sense," Elzeth said.

The man grinned. "Well, think on it, at least. You've got a while before you have to decide. I'll find you again before you leave and you can let me know what you think. But I hope we can cooperate. I'd hate to visit Angela one night. She seems nice."

Tomas's hand went to his sword, but before the blade was halfway from the sheath, the man had a dagger under his chin.

"I told you, Tomas. You're getting old."

Tomas sheathed his half-drawn sword. He'd often found nothing cooled the temper faster than having your ass handed to you in a fight, and his was as cold as ice right now.

The man sheathed his dagger. "I knew you were a reasonable man. Think about it, and I'll see you soon," he said as he left.

Tomas stood in the center of his room for a while, trying to wrap his head around what had just happened. Eventually, he collapsed onto the bed and stared at the ceiling.

"I really, really hate this town," Elzeth said.

U nfortunately, no matter how long Tomas stared at
the ceiling, it refused to answer the questions that
troubled him. As the sun kissed the tops of the neighboring
buildings, Tomas rolled off the bed.

"Going to see him?" Elzeth asked.

"Feel like it's going to be a long time before sleep finds
me, and I'm not much in the mood for being alone."

Tomas searched for unwanted company when he
stepped outside the inn. The streets were busier than he
expected for the time of day but not so busy an enemy could
hide in the crowd. Tomas stood and watched the flow of
people, ignoring the looks others shot his way. He didn't
forget to check roofs and windows, but he saw nothing that
concerned him. He struck out toward the southwest.

It didn't take long for the streets to grow quiet. The two
thoroughfares bustled with activity, and some of that
movement leaked onto nearby streets, but once Tomas
escaped the more commercial areas of Razin, peace
returned. Most of the houses he passed were new, and many
were large by the standards of the day. Space was cheaper

out here, which allowed new arrivals to build houses bigger than any they could afford in the east. Toys were scattered in yards and gardens were filled with food to help families carry through the winter months. Here and there, a homeowner was outside, tending to their house or garden. They welcomed him as he passed with a smile.

When he'd last visited, he'd already considered Razin as a town on the edge of being livable, its downsides offset by the considerable draw of Angela's presence. Now it was too crowded, but Tomas found he didn't mind as much as he would have a few years ago.

"I can't decide what you're thinking about," Elzeth complained. "I've never felt you this calm walking through a city."

"It's nicer than most. There's something good here that I'd hate to see ruined."

"We might not want to stay too long, then. Towns don't tend to do well after we've been around for a bit."

Tomas's chuckle was dark. "True."

Tomas stopped when they came out across from Ben's place. The former inquisitor and his wife had built an addition along the west side of the house since Tomas had left, and it looked like they had purchased an adjoining property and extended the yard. The enormous silver maple had somehow grown even larger in his absence, as had the platform built around it. Even from across the street, the property radiated the same sense of peace Tomas had felt when he'd first visited. The damage done when the church attacked seemed a distant memory.

The front gate hung open, which surprised Tomas a little. After the last attack, he thought Ben would reconsider his open-door ideas.

He walked right in. The yard was as quiet as he'd ever

seen it, though he didn't need sagani-aided hearing to listen in on the bedtime battles happening within the house. He climbed onto the porch, sat on one of the rocking chairs, and rocked back and forth while the children went to sleep.

Eventually, the front door opened, and Ben poked his head out. He smiled wide when he saw Tomas. "I wondered who might be out here. Give me a minute, and I'll come out to join you."

Tomas nodded, and Ben disappeared back into the house.

He listened to a bit more shuffling about, followed by the muted tones of the conversation Ben was no doubt having with his wife. Tomas didn't bother to listen in. He trusted Ben and Olena as much as he trusted anyone in this wicked world. Then he heard bottles being cracked open, and when Ben reemerged, he had two ales in his hands. The former inquisitor handed one to the host, who accepted it gratefully. They clinked bottles in a silent toast, and each took a long pull. Ben settled into the rocking chair beside Tomas with a sigh of contentment.

"It's been a while, and you've been all over the newspapers," Ben said.

Tomas looked over at Ben, surprised for the second time that night. He replayed Ben's comment, certain he'd missed something. But he hadn't. There'd been no judgment, no insinuation, and no anger within the statement. Just an open curiosity, an invitation to say more.

Tomas had spent so long trying to justify and explain the events at Chesterton, Ben's simple acceptance felt like a skilled swordsman breaking through his guard with a single move.

That lack of judgment humbled Tomas. It made him wish he could be more like the inquisitor he'd once hated so much. He realized he still had said nothing, and he nodded. "It's been a journey. You have time for a story?"

"All the time in the world."

Ben leaned back in his chair and closed his eyes. Tomas took another long sip of his ale, then launched into his story. He spoke of Chesterton and Narkissa, Ghosthands and Hardin, Ulva and Gavin, and all the rest. Ben let him speak without interruption, his eyes closed. At times, he'd bring the bottle to his lips, the only sign he was still awake. Tomas knew him well enough to understand that behind that façade, he was taking notes and memorizing Tomas's story.

An inquisitor never forgets, and that was doubly true of Ben.

When Tomas finally finished, Tolkin was high in the sky and the night was turning cool.

"You're right. That is quite the journey," Ben said. Once again, Tomas heard no trace of judgment in his voice. Ben's jaw moved as though he were chewing on a gristly piece of meat.

Some part of Tomas felt lighter, as if telling Ben the story had lifted some of the burdens that weighed him down.

"I—I feel lost," Tomas admitted. He finished the last of his ale and placed the bottle carefully next to the rocking chair. "I don't know where any of this ends. I can keep fighting the church until the end of my days, but I'm wondering if it's worth my time."

Ben only grunted.

"No advice?" Tomas asked.

"Seems to me I gave you plenty of advice the last time you visited, and it amounted to a whole lot of nothing."

"Doesn't mean you need to stop giving it."

Ben sighed and rubbed at his chin. "Also seems like the advice I'd give you, you aren't likely to appreciate much."

"I'd still hear it."

Ben shrugged, as if to say he'd warned Tomas, but Tomas was too bull-headed to listen. "I've thought a lot about your last visit, for obvious reasons. You're trying to atone for the sins of your past. Trying to do good to make up for the evil that's been done. In this, you and I are much the same, and I hope you believe me when I say that I understand. Thing is, though, what you're doing will never get you where you want to go."

"I don't follow."

Ben grimaced and scratched behind his ear. "Why do you think I run the orphanage?"

"To atone for your own sins."

Ben shook his head. "I thought about it that way once, and I was as grumpy as a hungover drunk listening to the mission bells pealing."

"What changed?"

"Well, most of it was Olena shouting some sense into me. But she made me realize there's no lasting peace in suffering for the sake of others. Martyrdom feels good for a bit, but it's no way to live. Olena told me that if I didn't enjoy working with the kids, we shouldn't do it. She gave me an ultimatum."

Ben finished the last of his ale and set his bottle down next to Tomas's. "I was furious for a bit, but she'd knocked something free in my mind. Made me realize something."

"What?" asked Tomas.

"That I'm running the orphanage because it's what I want to do. I love watching the children grow and learn. There's a spark in their eyes when they finally understand something I've been teaching them. I love watching them become strong people who can set out on their own and find their own path. It took me a bit to realize, but I'm here because I want to be."

"What does any of that have to do with me?"

Ben arched an eyebrow. "Are you fighting because it's what you really want to do?"

The question pierced Tomas like an arrow through the heart. "I was never looking for the fight. The fight found me."

Ben nodded with an expression that said he didn't believe it.

"So, you're saying I should just walk away from everything? If the church isn't stopped, there's no telling what they'll do!"

Ben made a *tsk* sound and shook his head. "That's a way of thinking that needs to go, too."

"How so?" Tomas snapped. He wasn't sure if the ale had hit him harder than he expected, but his patience wore thin.

"When you say, 'the church,' you're treating the entire organization and the tens of thousands of believers as one monolithic entity. When you say it needs to be stopped, it sounds like you want the whole thing to come crashing down."

"Don't you? More than almost anyone, you know the evils the church has committed."

"Of course. But I've also seen all the good, too. I've seen people find friends and partners because of the church. I've seen faith lead to hope and goodness when the world led only to darkness. Hells, it was because of all the good I'd seen that I committed the sins that I did. I told myself that defending what was good about the faith was worth the sins I stained my soul with."

Tomas had no patience for Ben's sermons. "Speak plainly, Ben. What are you trying to tell me?"

"Well, first, that you really need to figure out what you want and fight for that, instead of letting events keep batting you around. But second, I'm trying to tell you that the church isn't evil. There are people within it who are, absolutely, and they deserve the edge of a sword as much as anyone alive. But if your thought is to bring down the whole church, I can't help but think you'll be doing far more harm than good. Hells, it'll make your crimes during the war pale in comparison. The peace you seek will be farther out of reach than ever before."

Tomas didn't have to listen to this. He'd thought that Ben, of all people, would understand. He stood. "So what, you think I should start an orphanage?"

Ben met the fire of Tomas's anger with a cool gaze. He tapped his chest with a finger. "I think that if you want peace, start fighting what's in here instead of killing everything out here you blame for your problems."

The words cut like a rusted knife. If anyone should have understood Tomas's fight against the church, it was Ben. Tomas's anger burned hotter than ever. "Go to hell, old man."

Ben nodded. "I might. I do fear for my soul. But even if that awaits me on the other side of the gates, I hope I'll rest easier knowing that I spent my years after meeting you doing something I treasured with people I loved."

Tomas snarled and stomped off into the night.

He had no time for fools.

8

Quinton rode into Razin alone. He'd already gathered the knights from Baldwin, given them their instructions, and sent them on their way. They'd chafed at his orders, their pride as knights interfering with their common sense. They believed that taking off their uniforms shamed them, even though they became far more effective in the guise of travelers.

The priest at Baldwin had been a great help. She'd been in the area for years, and she knew more about Razin than had been in the files Quinton had read. Speaking with her had given him a better idea of the battlefield he was walking onto.

In short, the discovery and subsequent destruction of the research center had driven a stake through the heart of the church in Razin. Many believers tore the symbol of the church from their clothes and stopped attending services at the mission. Those who didn't believe harshly attacked the few believers whose faith still led them to the mission. The new priest in town was an outcast, shunned by all but a few.

What no one in the area knew, including the priest in

Baldwin, was that Razin's new priest was an inquisitor. Quinton couldn't quite guess at Father's logic, for it had been Father who ordered the inquisitor there, but he was grateful for the additional strength at hand.

He understood the knights' desire to ride into town, their heads held high, ready to retake Razin for the church. But he also understood the power of a mob. He'd used it against Tomas in Chesterton. He'd be damned if he allowed it to turn against him here. So the knights entered Razin in ones and twos, wearing dusty travel clothes that wouldn't attract unwanted attention.

The prisoner wasn't due to be transported for two more days. Part of Quinton was tempted to simply storm the marshal's office, break the scholar free, and leave Razin behind. He was nearly certain he had the resources to do so, and Father had made it clear he didn't care how much of a mess Quinton left behind in Razin. The town was already as good as dead to the church, and there was no harm in kicking a corpse.

He couldn't bring himself to take the straight path, though. A lifetime of service had taught him the value of care and discretion. A scalpel often accomplished more than a club with less effort. Information and planning were at the heart of any successful mission.

So, instead of charging straight to the marshal's office, he rented a room in the same inn the knights stayed at. Two were in the common room breaking their fast when he arrived, but Quinton paid them no mind. He dropped off his bags and left the inn.

He wandered the town with no particular destination in mind. The day was a busy one, and he noted what parts of the town were filled with people and which were quiet. He studied rooftops and alleys, committing everything to a map in his head that grew more detailed with every passing hour. His meandering route also gave him the opportunity to ensure he wasn't being followed.

When he was certain no one in town cared about him, he turned toward the mission. No one was watching it the way the marshals had in Baldwin, which made Quinton's life much easier. He walked straight in.

The priest hid the truth of his identity well. He was a young man, but small, and he affected a small limp as he approached Quinton. He looked more harmless than a fly, but Quinton suspected the priest's long sleeves hid the chained daggers so many inquisitors cherished.

"Greetings, friend," the priest said.

Quinton produced a sealed letter from a pocket and presented it to the priest. "Father sends his greetings."

The priest's face betrayed nothing as he ripped the seal and read the missive. When he looked back up, there was a newfound appreciation in his eyes. "It's truly good to see you," he said.

"Likewise. What can you tell me?"

"Not as much as I would like. The few true believers who remain in this town aren't in position to tell me much. All signs point to the departure of a posse the day after tomorrow. It sounds like an army unit will arrive tomorrow. They'll get one night of rest, then leave early in the morning. I haven't been able to learn anything from the marshal's office, though. The chief marshal, Angela, is efficient and keeps things quiet. Hard to learn much."

"Any ideas on the number of guards the transport will have?"

"Close to thirty, and the army is bringing trained rifles."

Quinton grimaced. He'd expected a fight, but those odds

were poor. "Does it make more sense to attack the marshals before the army arrives?"

"Probably, but the prison is no easy target. Angela was here when the research station was revealed, and she learned her lessons from that experience. The doors and walls are reinforced, and since the arrival of the scholar, she's posted guards around the building to form a perimeter. It's why they don't have a marshal posted outside the mission at the moment."

Quinton chewed on the information. "Is there anything else I should know?"

"I can't think of anything. But I also haven't been able to learn as much as I'd like."

"Thank you for your help. You're available to help if I call on you?"

"Of course."

Quinton took his leave, once again wandering around Razin to ensure he wasn't being followed. This time, he allowed himself to pass by the prison to confirm the inquisitor's information. As the false priest had claimed, the walls looked like they'd hold up to any attack short of dynamite, and he counted at least two guards with rifles on buildings across the street. A far easier task than taking on thirty rifles from the army, but not a simple one. And he'd need to find dynamite.

As he walked, he planned the assault. He was so lost in his thoughts he almost missed Tomas. When he finally registered the host, he had to check again to make sure he wasn't imagining things. Sometimes he saw Tomas in places he couldn't be, and a second check always stripped away the illusion.

But this time, Tomas was walking down an intersecting street, right toward him.

Only years of training kept Quinton from freezing in place. He'd worn a wide-brimmed hat to hide his face, and he tilted his head so Tomas wouldn't see him. He kept walking, then ducked around the next corner.

His heart was pounding in his chest and his breath came in shallow gasps.

Of course Tomas would be here. He was always in the place where he could most hurt the church, and Quinton's knowledge of the host's movements was weeks out of date.

None of that mattered now.

Tomas was here.

Quinton could kill him, and the church would lose one of its greatest enemies. He'd be able to rest at night, knowing he had finally atoned for his failures outside Chesterton.

He poked his head around the corner and watched as Tomas reached the intersection Quinton had just crossed. The host paused in the middle for a moment, gazing toward the prison. Quinton pondered the gesture and its possible meanings. His first assumption was that Tomas was cooperating with the marshals, but the host made no movement toward the office.

The moment passed, and Tomas continued in his previous direction. Whether or not he was cooperating with the marshals, he was alone now. Quinton let him pass out of sight, then followed. He stayed well back and kept as many people between him and Tomas as possible.

Tomas didn't seem worried about being followed. He didn't check behind him, and he made no sudden turns or stops that might force a pursuer to reveal their presence. He walked straight down most of the road and turned right.

Quinton clutched at the hilt of his sword and looked for the trap he was certain was waiting to close on him. The rooftops were empty, though, and no one paid him any special attention. He couldn't believe his fortune. It felt as though the Creator smiled at him from above. He had caught Tomas by surprise.

He hurried forward so as not to lose his prey, slowing at the corner Tomas had turned right on. His sharpened senses weren't much good this close to the center of Razin, but he didn't hear Tomas waiting in ambush. He poked his head around the corner just in time to see Tomas opening the main door to an inn. The host stepped inside and closed the door behind him without a second glance.

Quinton studied the inn from his vantage point. It was smaller and newer than the one he and the knights stayed at. It was only two stories tall, meaning that no matter where Tomas slept, he'd be able to escape easily. The inn wasn't an ideal place to attack. Tomas would know the layout better than him, and he couldn't risk exploring within and simply hope they didn't bump into one another. The wise play was to wait and gather more information.

But that came with its own risks. The longer the two of them were in town together, the more likely it became that Tomas learned of Quinton's presence. He knew he had the element of surprise now. It was too valuable to waste. He gripped his sword's hilt tightly, checked the area one more time for dangers, then strode toward the inn.

The closer he came, the more his steps faltered. What if all of this had been intentional, designed to lure Quinton into a trap? It was what Quinton had done to Tomas back in Chesterton.

And even after all his careful planning, Tomas had still escaped.

He wasn't an opponent Quinton could afford to underestimate. Once, he'd been certain that his strength was without equal. But reports from Kimson claimed that

Tomas had stood directly in the blast of the church's new cannon and lived to tell the tale. There was no telling how strong Tomas had become since they'd last crossed swords.

Quinton stopped across the street from the inn. He imagined himself kicking the front door opening, surprising Tomas, and cutting him down before he could unify with the demon within. The vision gave him the courage to take another step before he stopped again.

He was being a fool.

Tomas was the impulsive one. The host carried away by his emotions and guilt. Quinton moved with care and struck at the precise moment it would have the greatest effect.

A slight delay carried little risk. Only the false priest and the knights knew Quinton was in Razin, and he trusted them all with his life. He had time.

A slow smile spread across his face. He had been thinking about this all wrong. Tomas's presence in Razin wasn't an obstacle so much as it was yet another gift from the Creator. Quinton didn't know Angela or the marshals, so he couldn't predict how they would act. But he knew Tomas. Hells, he even knew Elzeth, the demon that had consumed Tomas's soul.

He would come up with a new plan.

One that would finish Tomas once and for all.

9

The conversation with Ben left Tomas so distracted that his arrival at the inn caught him by surprise. He couldn't remember any of the turns he'd taken to get here, nor anything about the city he'd passed through. He shook his head to clear it. It was foolish, walking through Razin with his attention wandering pretty much everywhere else. He was lucky no one had chosen that moment to strike.

The open common room tempted him with the promise of another ale, but he decided against it. He'd already had enough, and there was no telling when the church would strike. If he were in their position, he'd attack before the army arrived with the additional support. Angela had reinforced the prison well, but it was still an easier target than a highly trained unit of army veterans armed with rifles.

Tomas went up to his room but was too antsy to sit, and he didn't even dream of falling asleep. Ben's accusations mixed with his concerns about an impending attack, and he paced the room to rid himself of the troubling thoughts.

When that didn't work, he laid down on his bed and stared wide-eyed at the ceiling.

What he really wanted to do was return to the prison. So long as the scholar was there, that would be the center of attention. They needed him, even if they didn't realize it.

But Angela had been clear. She'd likely just order him to leave again.

A part of him thought he should go to the office, anyway. Angela didn't understand the forces arrayed against her the way he did, and it was possible that her feelings about him were coloring her judgment. Of course, he supposed she could easily say the same about him.

He interlaced his fingers behind his head and continued to stare up at the ceiling. If nothing else, he could show Angela the respect of following her directions.

His satisfaction at the decision did nothing to ease him to sleep. The world grew darker, but his eyes refused to close. Before they could, a low rumbling echoed between the walls of the buildings and through his open window.

Tomas sat bolt upright and looked out the window. His limited perspective gave him no clue what had happened, but he would recognize that sound anywhere, especially after his time with the 34th.

Someone had just used dynamite in town. And being as there were no coincidences, Tomas had a pretty good idea of what building had endured the explosion.

Still fully dressed, he came to his feet in a moment. He ignored the door because leaving through the main door of the inn would cost him precious moments. Elzeth burned, and Tomas went to the window, stepped up onto the ledge, and dropped. He landed softly on the road below, his knees flexing with the impact. He glanced left and right to see if anyone had observed his departure, and then he sprinted down the narrow lane.

The explosion had set off a commotion. Concerned citizens came to their windows and peered outside. From down another street, Tomas heard sounds of panic and pounding feet. He outran them all, and when he reached a larger intersection, he looked to the sky and saw smoke drifting up and blocking the light from the moon.

He took comfort in what he didn't hear. The clang of swords did not echo down the empty streets, and no rifles discharged their deadly load. Tomas dared to hope the damage was less than what he feared. After several blocks and a handful of turns, Tomas came out on the familiar street in front of the prison. Fires burned near the door, and it looked like the world's largest sagani had thrown a boulder against the front wall. But the building stood tall and seemed relatively unharmed.

Tomas's eyes narrowed. Someone had clearly used dynamite against the building, but where was the assault?

He looked up and down the street, even checking behind him to see if anyone fled from the destruction. But for the moment, the street looked quiet.

Then Tomas thought about the guards that Angela had stationed on the roofs on the other side of the prison. Their duty had been to prevent precisely something like this from happening. He glanced once again at the prison. Though it was damaged, it didn't appear to be in any immediate danger. He ran instead across the street to check on the guards.

He scrambled up the side of a building but stopped as soon as he pulled his head over the lip. There was a guard there, surrounded by a pool of his own blood. The rifle they'd been armed with sat in the same pool, unfired. Just from the amount of blood, Tomas was certain of what he would find, but he stepped gingerly onto the roof and inspected the body.

The marshal's neck had been slit from side to side with one quick, confident cut. Tomas couldn't have done it better. Tomas hopped over to the other roof, although he was already certain what he would find.

Once again, the guard was dead, and the blood trickled off the roof and down the drain spouts, which would funnel the blood straight into the street. This guard had just enough time to fight. There were defensive wounds on his arms, and his cause of death was a single stab wound through the heart.

Tomas stood from his examination. Most likely, he was only looking for one assailant. He imagined him surprising the first guard and killing the second before he could get a shot off. Then it was a simple matter to light a stick of dynamite, toss it across the street, and disappear before anyone was the wiser.

He frowned at the questions his story didn't answer. From where he stood, the attack had been wildly successful. So where was the assault?

He figured those were questions whose answers would have to come later. First, he needed to check on the marshals within the office. He needed to know that Angela was unharmed. He dropped back down onto the street and walked across.

A crowd of observers was gathering a ways away. So far, they were too timid to approach the scene. Tomas checked to make sure none of them were carrying rifles and was pleased to see none.

One look at the front wall told him he wouldn't be getting in that way. The dynamite had caved the wall and door in to where it would take a team of horses to pull the door on its hinges. Even that wasn't a sure bet.

Instead, Tomas ran around the back. The wall surrounding the practice yard was high, but with Elzeth's help, Tomas clambered up and over without a problem.

He stopped when he was perched on top of the wall. The practice grounds were empty, but there were two large windows that opened up from the prison into the space, and Tomas didn't want to be greeted by a hail of lead when he dropped into the yard. "It's Tomas," he shouted.

There was no answer or response.

"Please don't shoot."

Tomas waited a few moments more, then dropped into the practice yard. As soon as he landed, he held up his hands and inched forward. His sagani-aided hearing picked up the sounds of a commotion within the office, but no gunshots rang out, which he considered a great sign.

Before he could get to the door, it opened, and Angela poked her head out. "Tomas, what are you doing here?"

Tomas gestured toward the front of the building. "It sounded like you were having a party, and I was jealous you didn't invite me."

For a long moment, Angela stared daggers into him, and he wondered if beating a tactical retreat wasn't his wisest course of action. But then she shook her head and ran her hand through her hair. "You have any idea how close we came to shooting you?"

"Hopefully not very."

Her look told him he was lucky to be alive.

"Are you all okay in there?" Tomas asked.

"Shaken up. And I think one marshal is going to have a concussion from the way he fell. But otherwise, we're okay. What do you know about what happened?" she asked.

Tomas grimaced. From how she answered the question, she didn't yet know about her dead marshals. He wished he didn't have to be the one to deliver that news. "Not much. I was at the inn when I heard the explosion and rushed over here." He paused. "I'm sorry, but both of your marshals out front are dead. Looks like the work of one killer. Someone strong. Other than that, everything seems quiet. There's no trace of whoever did this."

Angela's eyes narrowed at that. He saw his questions reflected in her gaze. He could see that she wanted to ask but knew he didn't have any answers for her.

"I don't think it's safe to stay," he said.

"Where else would we go? This is the only hardened position for miles."

"And just before this, I was lying in bed thinking that if I was in the church's shoes, I'd attack you here before the army arrived, and that's not all. You've also got a problem with the Family who also wants the scholar locked up in their own cells."

She glared at him. "How do you know that?"

"One of them threatened me. Told me I was supposed to steal the scholar before the church could get their hands on her. Threatened you and Ben and the kids if I didn't."

She shook her head again. "How in the hells do you always bring so much trouble with you?"

"It's either a talent or a curse, but I'm leaning towards a curse."

"Agreed. So what are you thinking?"

Her decisiveness stirred feelings Tomas thought were best kept buried. Despite everything that had happened between them, she still trusted him. Even when he had admitted the Family had tried to coerce him. The thought restored the determination he hadn't even been aware that he had lost.

"We take her out, and we stay on the move. I'm guessing there's no place in Razin that's going to be safe. Our faces are too well known, and there aren't that many places to hide. So we take her outside of town, and we start our journey a few days early."

"What about the army?"

"All we have to do is to survive the two or three days until we can meet up with them. Once we do, I don't think there are any forces in the area strong enough to stop us."

"That's a terrible plan."

"Yeah, but I don't have one better. Do you?"

She shook her head. "You have no idea how much it pains me to admit that I don't."

Tomas forced a smile onto his face that he didn't feel. "See? We'll figure it out. As long as we've got the two of us, what could possibly go wrong?"

The shots of rifles echoed from the front of the building. Angela glared at him. "Now, why did you have to go and say something as dumb as that?"

10

————

Tomas interlaced his fingers to give Angela a place to put her foot. She placed her right boot in his hands and held onto his shoulders as he lifted her to the top of the wall. The scent of her filled his nostrils, and he breathed in deeply. The smell was familiar, like that of a favorite childhood meal. She smelled of dust and sweat mixed with the slightly floral scent of whatever soap she used.

Elzeth's strength allowed him to lift her without a problem, and she balanced on his hand with ease. She grabbed the lip of the wall and pulled herself up, pausing on the top, just as he had when he'd entered the practice yard. "You need any help?" she asked.

He shook his head, and she dropped carefully down the other side of the wall. He took a few steps back, then ran at and up the wall, dropping beside her.

The street in front of the prison was brighter than when he'd entered, and Tomas guessed quite the crowd had gathered. Fortunately, the gunshot hadn't been followed by many more, but it only took one to unleash chaos. Angela led the way toward the street while Tomas stayed close behind, hand on the hilt of his sword.

When they reached the street, they discovered a disaster in the making. One man, armed with two rifles, stood in front of the marshal's office. He was young, and his eyes were wide. One rifle pointed south down the street while the other wobbled in the general direction of north. A silver badge reflected Tolkin's dim light.

As Tomas had guessed, the brighter lights were evidence of a gathering crowd. The motley collection of citizens he'd ignored on his way to the prison had grown into the size of two small mobs, one in each direction. Many carried lanterns held high, and Tomas slipped briefly into the past, finding himself before the mob at Chesterton with innocents hanging from the tree.

"Tomas!" Angela's sharp rebuke brought him forcefully back to the present. He blinked away his memories and stared in confusion at the sword in his hand. It was his sword, as familiar to him as Elzeth's comforting presence. Past and present collided, and he had to squint to make sure the blade wasn't covered in blood.

Fortunately, it was clean.

"Tomas, what are you doing?" Angela's voice was laced with concern and something else. Something he couldn't remember ever hearing in her voice before, not even when the church had unleashed its hell on Razin before.

Fear.

Of him.

He shook his head to clear the last thoughts of Chesterton from his memories. Angela had turned toward him, as though he was the most dangerous threat on this street filled with wide-eyed baby marshals and an angry and worried mob.

He stammered a response, but there was no justifying his behavior. Some loved to brandish their swords to intimidate or make themselves feel stronger and braver than they were. None of that applied to Tomas. He drew his sword only to draw blood. Right now, he didn't even remember drawing it.

"Sorry," he said. He sheathed the blade, but Angela's eyes didn't leave him. Only after a long moment, when she could reassure herself he wasn't a danger, did she turn around. That lingering look cut him as deeply as any warrior he'd ever fought against.

"What's going on, Stephen?" Angela pointed the question at the young marshal standing with the two rifles.

"They're dead, boss. Both Michael and Percival. Blood's still on their rifles. They died protecting the prison, and I mean to do the same."

From the tone of Stephen's voice, Tomas believed the young man meant it, too. The kid was a damn fool, but he wasn't Tomas's problem. He turned his attention instead to the mob currently being held back by the twin rifles. No one in the crowd seemed overly suspicious. Most were still in their bedclothes, awakened by the explosion the same as he'd been. They were sleepy, curious, and a little afraid. Tomas counted perhaps a dozen swords in the crowd, but he was more concerned by the one rifle that had appeared. The man who carried it appeared to be a hunter. It was slung over his shoulder with a strap, so it didn't look like he would bring it to bear soon, but its presence was still concerning.

He stepped toward the crowd, intending to put himself between them and the over-matched marshals. An icy stare from Angela froze him in place. "What do you think you're doing?" she asked.

"Just going to help keep the crowd away."

Angela looked between the crowd, her marshal, and Tomas. Then she shook her head. "I could really use someone I trust watching the rear. Do you mind?"

The request felt like a punch to the stomach. Tomas stared, incredulous, but when she didn't back down, he gave her a curt bow, then walked stiffly back to the alley they'd just emerged from. He almost kept walking to the next street, where he could return to the inn. He was suddenly exhausted and terribly tempted to leave.

She'd used the rear entrance as an excuse to get rid of him, but she also wasn't wrong about the need. Now would be an excellent time to strike.

And his bow had served as a sort of promise. He wouldn't break his word to her, so he climbed the wall for the third time that night. A long bench ran along one wall for the practicing marshals to rest on. He walked over to it and slumped down.

"Sorry," Elzeth said.

"No more than I deserve. Still hurts, though." Tomas let the back of his head rest against the wall. It was still warm from the day's heat.

He heard a few raised voices from the front of the office, but he didn't ask Elzeth to burn any brighter so he could listen in. The young marshal and the crowd were her problems. He closed his eyes and let his attention wander to Elzeth simmering quietly near his stomach.

A troubling thought occurred to him. "You didn't cause me to draw my sword, did you?"

After a long pause, Elzeth said, "I don't think so."

"Not as reassuring as I'd hoped."

"Sorry. My own thoughts aren't as dependable as I'm used to."

Tomas looked down at his hands. He held them in the

air, and they were as stable as ever. "Wish I knew more of what was happening to us."

"You and me both."

Tomas rubbed his eyes. "You can rest for a while. I'll call if I need you."

Elzeth didn't argue, but Tomas noticed it took him longer to settle than it had in the past. Still, he was alone before long.

Tomas looked up to the sky, but the stars refused to answer him.

In time, the citizens of Razin brought ladders to help everyone scale the walls around the practice yard. Angela was the first to climb over and join Tomas, followed shortly thereafter by the young marshal who had so eagerly brandished the rifles out front.

The sight of her made Tomas's chest hurt, but he ignored the sensation. She issued orders, and those who'd joined her in the practice yard hopped to obey. She watched for a few moments, then approached Tomas. "We're going to evacuate most people from the prison. Then I'm putting the marshals on guard around the building while we talk. Will you wait here until I'm free?"

"Of course."

She gave him a strange look, then went into the jail with the rest.

As far as Tomas could see, the evacuation of the jail proceeded efficiently. Angela had clearly considered the details before beginning. She was, without a doubt, a much better marshal than he ever would have been. Not that anyone in the government ever would have asked him. They were too busy trying to execute him.

It wasn't long before they were once again alone in the practice yard. Angela rubbed the palms of her hands off on her pants, then sat down next to him. "We need to talk about Chesterton."

Tomas swallowed the stone that appeared in his throat. "What do you want to know?"

"Everything."

So, for the second time that night, Tomas told the story of the Chesterton Massacre, leaving nothing out. When he finished, Angela was silent for a good bit. Then she said, "That's quite the story."

Tomas sensed the smart choice was to remain silent, so he did.

Angela leaned back against the wall. "If we're going to leave here before the army arrives, I need to know that I can trust you completely."

Tomas nodded.

"Why did you draw your sword back there?"

Tomas blew out a sharp breath. "I don't know."

Her answering look was sharp. "You'll have to do better than that."

"Something is happening to Elzeth and me. It might be madness, but I'm not sure. I don't remember drawing my sword."

He thought he heard Angela's breath catch for a moment. Then she closed her eyes. "I'm sorry, Tomas. The prisoner stays here for now."

Tomas shot to his feet. "It's too dangerous!"

Angela slowly stood. "I don't disagree. But it's the right decision." She paused, looking for the right words. "I trust your intent, and you don't know how much I want you to help. But I can't."

Tomas growled and clenched his fists. He looked away, unable to face her. It had been a long time since he'd wanted to lash out, but anything he said would only make the situation worse.

"Fine," he snapped.

He was up and over the wall before she could call out after him.

11

_____

Quinton watched the scene unfold in front of the prison. He grinned in wicked delight when Tomas and Angela emerged from the alley. Tomas had his sword drawn, and when Angela noticed, she looked as though she was ready to arrest him. They argued for a bit, which ended with Tomas returning to the alley.

Quinton had always been a man who was proud of his work. That was a thread that ran through his days in the army to his service today. But when he saw Tomas shamed, a rush of almost childish glee ran through him. Of course, Tomas would struggle with mobs. If Angela was wise, she'd arrest him immediately, before Tomas snapped. Quinton almost giggled, but several long breaths allowed him to keep quiet. It wouldn't do to draw any attention to his hiding place.

He felt the hand of the Creator at his back, pushing him forward. Like everyone else in town, he'd heard the explosion and rushed to see the damage. Neither he nor any of his knights had set the dynamite. They mingled among the crowd, eager to witness any fresh developments with their own eyes.

Quinton had pursued a higher vantage point. He'd hidden himself upon a roof several buildings down the street. The demon within him granted him extraordinary eyesight, so the additional distance didn't rob him of any details. On the contrary, he could see almost everything that happened from where he lay.

It was a pleasure to watch Angela settle the crowd and reassure them. Had Quinton been more prepared, he might have instructed the knights to rile the crowd up, but he felt his opportunities weren't long in coming. Chaos was fertile soil for the seeds of his plans.

He burrowed deeper into the shadows that concealed him. The distraught marshal, whom Quinton had hoped would unload the barrels of his rifles into the bystanders, argued with Angela and pointed his right rifle to the roof a few buildings away. Quinton had noted the guards earlier in the day and now noticed how still and silent those rooftops were. Whoever had left the dynamite had left some bodies behind, too, it seemed.

Angela called for a group of volunteers to retrieve the bodies. Quinton grew perfectly still as concerned citizens clambered up the buildings to help. One wary glance in his direction threatened to bring a load of trouble down on his head. Hiding as he was, it was easy to imagine the blame placed on his shoulders, though this once he was innocent.

The thought of being persecuted for another's crimes threatened another outburst of giggles.

Quinton frowned. This wasn't like him. He'd been pushing himself hard, and he might need rest. Once there was time, he promised himself he'd nap.

Fortunately, no one looked his way. The dead bodies

consumed everyone's attention. Quinton listened to mutterings of disbelief and a few choked sobs from those who knew the deceased marshals best. But everyone in the crowd realized that whatever had happened was over, and given the hour, many were eager to return to their beds. The volunteers lowered the bodies to the street, and the crowd gathered around.

Quinton waited in hiding, troubled by the questions he couldn't answer. Who had left the explosive outside the marshal's office and why? Outside of killing the two marshals, the attack didn't seem like it had accomplished anything.

Eventually, the excitement below died down, and the crowd dispersed back to their homes. A handful brought ladders and helped those trapped within the prison to escape out the rear. Most of the remaining marshals set up a laughable perimeter to protect the office. That made Quinton suspect their scholar was still in the prison.

Should he attack? The prison would never be as vulnerable and unprepared as it was now.

The knights, lacking direct instructions, wandered back to the inn as the crowd returned to their homes. Quinton remained on the roof, carefully weighing his options. If not for Tomas, the decision would be a simple one.

He was about to abandon the roof when there was movement from the alley. Tomas emerged with his head down. He looked like a child who'd just had a treat stolen.

Quinton stilled himself and watched. If Tomas looked up, Quinton wasn't sure he'd escape notice.

Fortunately, Tomas was less interested in his surroundings than a drunk with two ales before him. The host's gaze never left his feet, which shuffled down the street as though they were weighted with stones.

The sight was almost enough to tempt Quinton into attacking. But as before, he hesitated. Was this some sort of trick, a way to bait Quinton into revealing himself? All his senses argued otherwise, but he didn't trust them. He watched Tomas walk down the street and turn the corner, apparently oblivious to anything around him.

When Quinton was sure it was safe, he dropped from his roof to the ground below. Though it pained him, Tomas wasn't the reason he was here. The scholar was as unprotected as she was going to be. He almost strode toward the prison but decided not to be a fool. It would only take a bit to summon the knights and attack together. This mission was too important to leave to chance. He hurried to the inn.

Fortunately, the knights were up and in the common room. Most sat alone, spread apart so as not to invite suspicion. Quinton made a subtle sign as he entered, then went to his private room. They would leave the common room in ones and twos, and he patiently waited. Before long, they were all gathered.

He started without preamble. "Tonight is the night. I'm not sure who left the dynamite outside the prison, but it seems clear there's a third party interested in our scholar. Thanks to their efforts, the marshals are distracted and vulnerable. There's no point in waiting."

They hammered out a plan quickly. It wasn't complicated. They would approach the building from different directions and eliminate the guards at the same time. Two of the knights would lead the assault while Quinton and the others stood watch on the walls.

The knights asked good questions, but the meeting didn't last long. They were as eager as Quinton to finish the task they'd come here for. As soon as everyone was certain of their roles, they left the inn in ones and twos and returned to the marshal's office via varied routes. Quinton and two other knights approached from a side street, and Quinton was the first in their group to poke his head around a corner to study the terrain.

He grunted softly at the sight. The perimeter of marshals around the office had vanished. He signaled the knights behind him to wait while he watched. The street in front of the prison remained stubbornly empty. Had Angela given them the rest of the night off, thinking the danger had passed? Or had she brought them in so they could be more effective guarding the door? Everything he'd read about her led him to believe in her competence, so he doubted the marshals had disappeared.

It didn't much matter. With the knights at his back, they could have taken down a prison with four times as many guards. He gave the sign to advance.

The knights spread out according to the plan they'd established, and Quinton was put in mind of a hand, each finger operating in cooperation with its neighbors to accomplish remarkable feats.

Baldwin's knights were well-trained, as were all knights, but they were veterans, too. When they moved, they felt like extensions of Quinton's will. His life only sometimes intersected with knights, but when it did, he sometimes imagined leading them the way he did this night.

Right now, it felt as natural as breathing. Their advance raised no warnings, and Quinton's study of the nearby rooftops revealed no movement that would betray an ambush.

They met up again by the walls which surrounded the practice grounds. Quinton took up his position on top of the wall while two of the knights dropped like wraiths into the practice grounds.

Their arrival still didn't provoke a response from within the prison, and Quinton frowned. Several windows looked out over the grounds, and he didn't believe for a moment that the marshals would sit quietly while knights invaded their space. He whistled and held up his hand. The two knights stopped.

Something wasn't right. His stomach sank.

Had Angela moved the scholar in the brief window of time between when he'd left his post and returned with his knights?

He should have known better. He'd even felt the push of the Creator, and he'd ignored it. Cursing his foolishness, he waved the knights forward. The building was almost certainly empty, but he would be twice a fool not to investigate.

The knights nodded, then went to the door. One tested the handle.

Locked.

They'd come prepared, though. One knight slid a small sack of tools from his pocket and went to work on the lock. The click of the lock surrendering to the knight's assault was audible even from the wall. Quinton grimaced, but he suspected it wouldn't matter much. Angela had only locked the door behind her as she left.

The knight opened the door quickly and stepped in, sword drawn.

Quinton frowned as he heard something hissing from inside the prison. It was a familiar sound, but not one he'd heard in some time.

Realization dawned a few moments too late.

For the second time that night, an explosion rocked Razin.

12

Tomas sat upright in his bed for the second time that night. The sound of another explosion echoed through his window. As before, he hadn't been asleep. Angela's repeated rejections kept him up more effectively than tea ever had. Now he wondered if he'd ever fall asleep tonight.

"What in the hells is wrong with this city? Is everyone wandering around with dynamite?" Elzeth asked.

Tomas's thoughts had traveled in much the same direction. He threw on his pants, shirt, and boots. He looked to the window, then shook his head. The innkeeper had already been confused enough when Tomas had returned without leaving through the front door. He descended the stairs, waved a farewell to the worried innkeeper, then hurried down the street.

Once again, smoke and debris rose from the direction of the prison. This time, he couldn't bring himself to run toward the trouble. He was tired, and Angela had made it clear he wasn't particularly welcome. He couldn't hear any sounds of further fighting, so whatever had happened was already done. If not for his curiosity, he would have stayed in bed.

He joined the crowd of bleary-eyed citizens shuffling toward the prison. When they turned the corner and saw the destruction, many stopped to stare and whisper to their neighbors. Tomas ignored them and pushed through.

The prison was gone. Thick timbers and iron bars had been thrown outward, and the roof had collapsed like a giant boulder had fallen from the sky and flattened it. Tomas studied the damage for a bit. The explosion looked like it had come from within the building, but how? Had an attacker gotten in?

He didn't see any blood or limbs nor hear any cries for help. The guards that had been on duty were nowhere to be found. It was strangely quiet.

Tomas's thoughts were sluggish. His thoughts kept turning to bed and a good night's rest. Nothing about this night and this town made sense. But he forced himself to stare, to observe and note the details that would explain the story of this night's excitement.

The sight of the prison brought forth an old memory. During the war, both sides had hotly contested several of the major rivers out east. Riverboats had become precious commodities, targeted by everyone and guarded jealously. Once Tomas had been on a doomed riverboat facing half a dozen attacking craft. Instead of ceding the valuable transport to the enemy, the captain had scuttled the ship. He'd ordered soldiers to crack the hull with axes and swords, then swim to shore.

The prison reminded Tomas of that decision. There were no guards, no blood, and the walls were blown outward. Had Angela scuttled the prison like the captain had scuttled his ship? Maybe, but he couldn't think through the logic of the choice.

Hells, he was tired. He rubbed at his eyes.

"Maybe you shouldn't worry," Elzeth said.

"Why not?"

"I'm just thinking about what Ben told you and how you reacted. You don't really want to fight, and it seems to me you've got a battle here where no one is much interested in you. Maybe that's not a bad thing. Maybe just this once, we sit it out and let someone else worry."

Tomas acknowledged the temptation. He wanted Angela more than he wanted this fight, but it looked like both were slipping from his grasp. He couldn't let himself off the hook that easily, though. "It matters if they're fighting over a scholar who thinks she can control the nexuses. If that's not worth fighting for, I don't know what is."

The sagani went quiet at that. Tomas appreciated having the silence to think. His hand went up to his chest, where he felt the key to her house through his shirt. She wouldn't have gone to her house. If she believed she was in danger, it was far too obvious a destination. But she might have left something there for him.

It was a stretch. He wasn't sure if she wanted him anywhere near what was happening. But it was the only lead he had. The alternative was to surrender, return to his inn, fall asleep, and see what happened.

He left the crowd behind and walked toward her house. As much as Razin had grown, he remembered the route. He checked behind him and let his gaze travel along the rooftops, but he saw no one following.

At her back door, he checked again for pursuit, but the night was quiet. He took the key out from under his shirt and pulled the chain over his head. He held his breath as he stuck the key in the door. It turned easily.

The door opened on silent hinges, and he let himself in. Tolkin was almost straight overhead, allowing only diffuse light through the windows. The curtains were all drawn back. With his sagani-aided vision, Tomas might as well have entered the home in the middle of the day. It was quiet within, but Tomas caught whiffs of the same floral scent he'd smelled back at the prison. The same smell permeated every corner of the house.

He was tempted to call her name but held back. It didn't feel like she was here. He couldn't hear anyone breathing, and the only sounds of wood creaking came from beneath his own weight. He walked down the hallway, wary but unconcerned.

Around the corner was the kitchen and dining room. As soon as he entered, he found a familiar figure, perfectly still, sitting on one chair. His tattoos were visible, and his hair was so white it almost glowed.

"I'm disappointed, Tomas. I'm starting to think you aren't taking my threats seriously," he said.

"Where's Angela?" Tomas asked.

The Family assassin tilted his head toward the table, where a letter lay open. "According to that, they've left town to escape their pursuit. She's hoping you join them. Sounds desperate, even."

"Where?"

The assassin shrugged. "She drew a map. Easier to look at than try to describe."

"Then why not just grab the scholar yourself? From what I've seen, you're strong enough."

The blonde-haired man's answering smile was

enigmatic. "Because the point isn't for me to kidnap the scholar. It's for you to do so."

"Why?"

The other man stood. "You have two days. If you haven't delivered the scholar by then, I'll make good on my threat. Maybe I'll start with Olena. Or one of Ben's kids. There's so many of them there these days, and the fool still lets them come and go as they please. A terrible idea in such a dangerous world, don't you think?"

The assassin took a step toward the door, and Tomas attacked. Elzeth burned within, and in two quick steps, he drew his sword and struck.

Except the assassin wasn't where he was supposed to be. He danced away from Tomas's sword, then darted in behind it, daggers flashing. Tomas retreated, then got his sword between them. He advanced again, the tip of his sword a blur as he cut. The assassin slid out of the way of most of the strikes, only using his dagger when it was necessary.

They shuffled back and forth, neither gaining the advantage they sought. After another handful of passes, the assassin broke off from the fight, daggers still raised and ready. "I already told you that you can't kill me. If you attack again, I might have to get serious."

Tomas didn't doubt the assassin. He and Elzeth were short of complete unity, but not by much. He didn't feel like he'd posed any actual threat to the assassin. The thought of unity still terrified him, but no options remained.

"What do you think?" he asked Elzeth.

It felt like Elzeth was silent for a long time, though only a second or two had passed. Elzeth grunted, and that grunt carried months of argument behind it. After Kimson, they'd sworn that they would avoid unity, if possible.

But sometimes, there was no choice. Elzeth's grunt

acknowledged as much. The sagani was as terrified as Tomas, but like two friends daring each other to jump off a cliff into a river below, neither would back down.

Tomas grunted in return. "Yeah, I feel about the same." He reached into his pocket and let the small gemstone drop from the handkerchief he kept it wrapped in. A final trick, if he needed one.

The walls that stood between him and Elzeth dropped. Thoughts, fears, and logic vanished. He attacked and took pleasure in the wide eyes of his opponent. His sword reached out for the assassin as though it had moved on its own. The assassin stepped back, but he was too slow.

Tomas grinned triumphantly as he cut again.

Once again, the assassin evaded, now as fast as Tomas. Tomas frowned but had no time to react as the assassin took advantage of the missed cut. He broke Tomas's guard, driving his daggers into Tomas's arms and shoulders. His sword fell out of hands that refused to grip. The assassin reached behind Tomas and pulled his head down as he drove a knee deep into Tomas's stomach.

All the air left Tomas's lungs. He collapsed to the ground like a sack of flour someone had thrown. His sword lay within easy reach, but his arms refused to move. He was bleeding all over Angela's floor and thought she'd be furious to see how he'd ruined her tidy home.

The assassin squatted down beside Tomas. "I don't begrudge you trying to kill me. I've been waiting for it, really. But you can't beat me."

Tomas groaned.

"Now, I've done all the hard work for you. I was the one who threw the first dynamite and killed those pathetic marshals standing guard. It got Angela to realize the danger she was in. The church attacked tonight, you know. But the marshals were already gone, thanks to my warning. Now they're out in the open, so taking the scholar should be as easy as eating a slice of pie. Two days. Otherwise, I'm going to start feeding children to my daggers, and they're getting hungry."

Without another word, he left Tomas behind in a pool of his own blood.

13

Tomas groaned as blood trickled from his wounds. None of them were deep, and none were close to major blood vessels. Each had been placed with deliberate care, designed to incapacitate but not to kill. Considering he'd been at full unity when the blows had been delivered, the wounds were a statement of how much skill and speed separated him from the Family assassin.

Receding footsteps echoed from the hallway, a door opened and closed, and Tomas was alone.

He felt terrible for bleeding over Angela's floor, but it felt as though someone had rolled a pile of stones on top of him. He flopped over onto his back. "You good?" he asked.

"Yeah, but it'll take a while to heal," Elzeth said.

All things considered, Tomas didn't mind. Though they'd lost, they'd been unified, and they hadn't lost themselves. It was a small victory, but a victory nonetheless.

"I think I'm going to get some rest," he said.

"Here?" The sagani relented. He could feel Tomas's exhaustion as though it were his own. "I suppose it is getting late. Past your bedtime and all."

Tomas was asleep before he could retort. Nightmares haunted his sleep, chasing him the way a patient hunter pursues wary prey. Visions of various disasters played for him. In one, they gutted Angela before his eyes. Once that horror faded, Tomas slipped into another vision where he stumbled upon the bloody aftermath of an assault on Ben and Olena's place. In yet another, all the sagani across the continent died.

He woke in a cold sweat. Despite the poor quality of his sleep, it had still done wonders for his body. Elzeth had healed up his wounds, leaving only a fresh set of narrow scars. Tomas held up his hands. He made them into fists, then stretched his fingers out wide. They were steady and felt strong. As usual, Elzeth's work was beyond reproach.

"How are you feeling?" he asked.

There was no response. Tomas didn't feel even the slightest stirring in his stomach.

"Elzeth?"

Still nothing.

"Elzeth!" Tomas almost shouted the question out loud.

Finally, he felt the barest hint of activity as the sagani shifted. "What?"

Elzeth's voice sounded both sleepy and distant. Tomas's heart raced. "Are you hurt? What happened?"

"I'm fine." Elzeth sounded confused. "Why?"

"Been calling you for a bit. Couldn't feel you at all."

"Huh." Tomas felt the concern brewing within Elzeth, but it was a faint strain buried under a blanket of exhaustion.

"Get some rest. With any luck, we shouldn't need you for a while."

He pushed himself off the floor and looked around. He'd lost a decent amount of blood before Elzeth had sealed his wounds, and he felt guilty for staining Angela's floor. But it seemed foolish to take the time to clean up. He quickly wet a rag and wiped as much as he could but called it good after only a little work. Then he went to the table and stared at the map.

He laughed when he saw her destination. It was the same farmhouse the church and Family had used to guard the research station when he'd last visited. He suspected the marshals had repossessed it after the destruction of the station, making it an ideal waypoint. Though he remembered the way, he took the map, folded it, and stuffed it in his pocket. No need to leave it out for anyone to see.

When he put the paper in his pocket, he felt the pull of the small nexus hidden within. Last night, he hadn't even had the chance to use it.

And now he'd almost accidentally brushed up against it. The surprise of the contact might have been strong enough to pull him and Elzeth apart. He gingerly pulled the handkerchief out of his pocket, then folded it a few times. When the cloth was thick enough, he reached in with it to pick up the nexus and wrap it tightly. Then he returned the nexus to his pocket. He was glad Gavan had trusted him with the shard but sometimes wished he didn't have to bear the risks associated with it.

His stomach rumbled, and he offered Angela another apology. He raided through her food and ate his fill.

When he was finally ready, he left through the back door, locking it behind him. He kept his senses sharp, but no one paid him any special attention. The events of the previous night were the talk of the town, with guesses ranging from the possible to the incredible.

Tomas tested his own theories as he walked. The assassin had revealed much, and the situation was worse than Tomas had expected. He was particularly concerned the church was here, and he hadn't known. Given the importance everyone seemed to place on this scholar, they would have sent knights, at least.

Or worse.

He hurried out of town, breathing a sigh of relief when he put the buildings behind him. He hadn't been able to shake the feeling that there was a danger behind every corner, that every rooftop held a potential assassin. The prairies could, too, but Tomas trusted his senses more outside the city.

The trip to the farmhouse passed without incident. Tomas kept checking behind him, but the prairie was empty. He saw nothing but windswept grasses as far as the eye could see.

He reached the farmhouse well after noon. He approached with his hands raised, and he saw movement in the windows. As he neared, Angela stepped out. The sight of her released a knot that had been tight in his stomach. "I'm glad to see you alive. I was worried," he said.

There was a set of chairs on the porch. She sat down on one and invited Tomas to join her. "I figured the dynamite was meant to get us to move from the prison, but I left behind a trap for anyone who got too curious. Sounds like I was right in doing so."

"Risky move."

Angela shrugged. "It didn't seem like there were many safe moves to choose from."

"True enough. Any idea who triggered your trap?"

"No, but I'd love to know. Maybe the Family?"

"I don't think so. The Family assassin found me again last night. He told me he was the one behind the first attack, for exactly the reasons you guessed. Said it would make it easier for me to take the scholar from you. He implied it was the church that got caught by your trap," Tomas said.

Angela's look was suspicious. She seemed less interested in the church than in him. "Well, the assassin was right about it being easier for you. Is that your plan?"

Her distrust still stung. "Not my plan, but I need a better one, fast. He's holding you, Ben, Olena, and the kids hostage."

Angela looked around. "I'm a hostage? Because that's news to me."

"He's good, Angela. He's beaten me twice since I've gotten here. I can't protect you."

"I don't need your protection."

Tomas gave her a look.

She blew out a harsh breath. "Sorry. You're right. But I don't need you watching over me all the time."

"I know. But I need to kill him. He's only given me two days, and I couldn't live with myself if any harm came to you or the kids because of me."

Angela thought, then said, "We might have some other options."

She stood up, and Tomas gave her a questioning look.

She went to the front door. "I think it's time for you to meet the scholar everyone's tripping over themselves to possess."

That piqued Tomas's curiosity. He'd been wondering about the scholar and the amount of trouble one person had created. All he knew about her was that the marshals wanted her for murder, and she knew enough about the nexuses that the army, church, and Family were all salivating over the idea of her working for them.

They entered the hallway, which still hadn't been cleaned since Tomas's fight. The bloodstains gave the house an eerie feeling, even as sunlight poured through the windows. Angela walked to the back of the house, turned down another hallway, then stopped outside a door with a marshal stationed outside. She knocked. "Rachel, are you awake?"

"Yeah."

Angela opened the door, and Tomas followed her in.

He didn't know many scholars, but he assumed they were pale from lack of sun and nearsighted from all their time spent with their noses in books. Rachel surprised him on all counts. She was small, but as she stood to greet them, Tomas noted the ease and grace of her movements. Her hair was long and blond. It fell beneath her shoulder blades even though it was braided tightly.

Rachel was younger than Tomas had expected, and she looked between Tomas and Angela with a sort of wide-eyed curiosity, as though they were the most interesting people in her world. She didn't strike him as a murderer. When they'd entered, she'd been working at a table. Tomas glanced at her script and saw a line of beautiful, flowing letters.

Before he could read them, introductions were in order. Tomas bowed, and Rachel's eyes went a little wider when she heard his name. "You're him, aren't you? The longest-lived host on record."

"Yes, ma'am. At least I've yet to meet anyone who's been one longer."

"I have so many questions. Our records show that when you first became a host, you refused to use your new strength often. Do you think that has aided your longevity?"

The sudden inquiry left Tomas at a loss for words, but Angela interposed herself between them. "Rachel, if all goes according to plan, you'll have plenty of time to talk to Tomas, but for right now, we need to talk about you."

Rachel's disappointment only lasted for a moment, and then she was smiling again. She sat down on the edge of her bed and looked up at them expectantly. "Of course. Anything I can do to help."

Tomas glanced around the room. If his memory of the place served, this was one of the larger spaces, and it looked like she had it all to herself. The door was guarded, and Tomas heard another two sets of footsteps above, but none of the marshals seemed concerned about her escaping.

Before he could ask, Angela answered the question. "When we picked Rachel up, it was because she was wanted for several crimes. But now that we've talked to her, there's a lot more to her story than we first knew. I think you should listen to it, too, because it might help us out."

Angela pulled up a chair. "If you wouldn't mind telling us the story again. I think this will be the last time."

Rachel brushed a loose strand of hair out of her eyes and tucked it behind her ear. "I don't mind at all. If it can help you, I'm happy to tell it as many times as I need." She looked up at Tomas. "You might want to sit down, as it's a bit of a long story."

Tomas pulled up another chair and nodded.

"Right," Rachel said. "Well, to tell the story properly, I'll need to tell you at least a little about my childhood because it all leads me to today."

With that, Rachel launched into her story, and Tomas listened closely.

RACHEL'S STORY

"I'm still not sure about this," Mother said. She looked down at Rachel, who had her face in a book and was pretending to be completely entranced by the words and pictures within. In truth, she was listening closely to every word that passed between her parents.

"She's a curious child, and this will be something that very few people have seen. I think it will be a tremendous inspiration for her," Father said.

Rachel didn't think her act fooled Father. He always played along, but he saw and heard everything. Mother said it was what made him a brilliant scholar. Regardless, he did nothing to send her away while they argued, for which she was grateful.

"But it doesn't feel safe," Mother protested.

Rachel could almost hear Father's grin widen. "Of course not! But look carefully at the language you just used. You said it doesn't *feel* safe. And you're right. Even though I've seen it a half-dozen times now, my heart still pounds in my chest every time I see it. But every study we've ever run on it tells us it's completely safe, and it's truly a wonder."

Mother said nothing, but her disapproval could be felt in every corner of their small room. The train rumbled forward, and Rachel dared to look up. Despite Mother's arguments, it was already too late. They were on the way. "How much longer, Father?"

Father looked out the window. The tall buildings of the city gave way to shorter homes only a story or two tall. Rachel hadn't seen so much sky in several months.

"Not long now," he said. A grin spread across his face. "Are you excited?"

"Very much. Thank you for inviting us."

Mother grunted but said nothing.

Father's prediction turned out to be accurate, as they usually were. The train slowed to a stop less than an hour later, and they stepped off. Mother fiddled with Rachel's dress until she was certain it looked right. Rachel smiled, puffing out her chest a little to display the three wavy lines of the church crest. Mother had made it especially for the day.

They were greeted by several priests, who welcomed Father with smiles and open arms. The priests ushered the family into a carriage. Rachel marveled at the stuffed cushions and the comfortable ride. She was just getting bored by the luxury when they arrived at a small building in the middle of nowhere.

The building itself barely deserved remark. Rachel took one look at it and decided it was the ugliest building she'd ever seen. It was a squat, windowless cube with one door. Two large men with stony faces guarded the entrance. She looked up at Father, who stared eagerly out the carriage window.

The family disembarked, and the priests guided them to the entrance. The guards said nothing as the priests opened the door wide and led Rachel and her family within.

The small space was well-lit by lanterns. A few bunk beds had been pushed against one wall. There was a small stove and a table and chairs nearby. Rachel guessed that somewhere between four and six people called this nightmare of a building their home. She couldn't imagine living in a place like this, but she didn't think about it for long.

The living accommodations weren't nearly as interesting as what waited at the end of the room. There, a tunnel dug in the ground glowed with an otherworldly blue light. Rachel drifted away from the adults and toward the entrance to the tunnel. A steep and haphazardly constructed set of wooden stairs led down, and only Mother's hand on her shoulder prevented her from running down and exploring.

It took too long, but eventually, the adults led the way down the stairs. Mother held on tightly to Rachel's hand, but Rachel thought it was more for Mother's sake than her own.

When the source of the light came into view, Rachel stopped to stare. It was a stone, but nothing like the rocks Father sometimes brought home from his travels. This one shone with the blue light that seemed more vivid and more alive than any light she'd seen before. As it danced across her skin, she felt as though it was a warm caress.

The adults advanced far too slowly. They seemed more interested in talking about the stone than studying it.

Finally, Rachel could take no more. She twisted out of Mother's grip and gave in to the pull of the stone. She reached out her hand and touched it.

The world seemed to fall away. Adults shouted at her,

but their concerns hardly mattered. The stone was warm to the touch, like a pair of mittens left too long in the sun. The warmth wrapped her in a protective embrace and welcomed her like an old friend. Instead of the sound of concerned parents, a softer, subtler song filled her ears.

It was, without doubt, the most incredible experience of her life.

By the time the adults had finally pulled her away, the purpose of her life had been determined.

Twenty years later, Rachel rubbed at her eyes and shuffled the papers on her desk. Each was filled with her small, neat handwriting, detailing the experiences and information dozens of subjects had related. A knock on the door to her office startled her. A glance out the window confirmed it was incredibly late.

She stood, stretched out muscles that had gotten stiff from sitting, then answered the door. A balding man with round glasses stood outside, his hand raised as though he was about to knock again. He was smiling, but the smile unsettled her. Her impression was that this was a man who had long ago realized life was easier to navigate with a smile but didn't realize it was supposed to reflect an inner joy. His smile was a meaningless mask. The three waves of the church were stitched onto his coat.

He gave a quick bow, as empty of meaning as his smile. "Doctor."

"I'm sorry, I'm afraid you have me at a loss, Mr.—"

"Names aren't important. What is important is your research."

"My research?"

"You've been studying the nexuses for years, have you not? All generously funded by the church?"

She nodded.

"There are those in the church who are quite enamored of your theories about the nexuses, and they'd like to invite you to join a special research team we're creating. The position would require moving farther west, but rest assured, you would be well-compensated for your trouble."

Rachel blinked, wondering if she'd fallen asleep and was dreaming. "What kind of research?"

"Why, into the truth, of course. There are a handful of scholars who we feel are close to finally unlocking the secrets of the nexuses. We've got access to several stones, as well as hosts and new inventions that have furthered our knowledge. We want to make one last concerted push to find the truth, and we want you to be part of it. It's a project that has the direct support of the Father himself."

Rachel's heart raced. She cared little about the church. The faith of her parents had never meant much to her, but claiming their beliefs allowed her the greatest access to the nexuses. She'd spent years fighting for more access, more funding, and better tools. She'd made incremental progress, but it wasn't enough, not when success felt so close.

"Would it be safe to assume you're interested? I'd like to proceed as though your participation is certain," he asked.

Though the offer had come out of the blue, there was no doubt in Rachel's mind.

"I'm very much interested. How soon would you like me?"

"As soon as possible, doctor. It is becoming essential that we solve the riddle of the nexuses once and for all."

∽

Years passed as though they were days. Everything the visitor had promised that night had been delivered, and far more besides. Rachel and the others learned more about the nexuses in those years than she had in a lifetime of study before. She started as an assistant researcher on the team, then advanced to being one of the head researchers. Her contributions were valued.

After three years in that role, their lead scholar passed away from a sudden illness. At least, that was what the church told Rachel, and she found no reason to doubt their account. They invited her to take his place, and that was how she found herself as the head of one of the church's top labs dedicated to understanding the nexuses.

The day she officially began, she received an unusual visit. She was used to officials from the church coming and going as they pleased, but this visitor was different. He wore a sword on his hip, and he carried himself with the same attitude she associated with knights. He wasn't a knight, though. She saw he wore no insignia, and he didn't seem the type to take orders. He was something else, though he did not explain his role in the organization. He reeked of authority, though.

They met over tea in her office. "Congratulations on the new role, ma'am," he said.

He didn't even offer his name.

"Thank you. I'm still getting settled in, but it's exciting to be leading some of the best minds this generation has seen."

"We're all keen to follow your progress. It is because of your promotion that I'm here today. As the lead scholar for this team, you're going to be exposed to information only known to small circles of people within the church. Before you can be granted access to the information, I need to ask you a few questions."

"Is this some sort of test?" Rachel asked.

The man didn't deny it. "From what I've read, I think you understand this already, but it needs to be said out loud. The church will go to any length to understand the nexuses and their connection to the sagani. It is likely the stones are the creation of devils meant to undermine the Creator himself. To that end, there is nothing we won't do to learn the truth. Nothing at all."

Rachel's stomach fluttered, but she kept her face blank. "How can I help?"

"By continuing in your work and suggesting new directions for our research. I am here because there is no way for us to hide our methods from someone in your position. In the past, some scholars have been... reticent to go as far as is necessary for answers. I need to know you were the right choice for this position."

"What do you need to know?"

"As you know, several of our experiments involve hosts. Many are cooperative and willing to help for food and money. Others are less cooperative. Do you have any problem with that?"

The question didn't even require her to think. Their best information came from the hosts, and almost all were criminals. "Of course. Once they make their pact with the devils, they aren't human anymore. Experimenting on them is the only way for them to serve the Creator."

The man nodded. "Would you feel the same, no matter what form the host takes? Sometimes the demons possess children and the elderly against their will."

"And that's a tragedy, but it doesn't change the facts. If anything, a wider range of hosts provides us with more valuable data."

The man smiled, delighted. "We weren't wrong in

choosing you. I can see that now. A messenger will come by this afternoon with a large stack of files detailing all the experiments we've been running. Please be familiar with them by the end of the week. When you're done with them, burn them."

"As the Creator wills," Rachel said.

"As the Creator wills," the man agreed.

14

If Angela had thought that listening to Rachel's story would make her more sympathetic to him, she'd terribly misjudged him. Tomas listened to Rachel's story with as much politeness as he could muster, but it was hard to listen without drawing his sword and ending it prematurely. The scholar didn't seem like much, and he suspected that in a battle, she would be less useful than a butter knife, but she was probably responsible for the death of more hosts than any battle fought in the last three decades.

Her story slowed to a halt after she spoke of the meeting between her and the mysterious warrior. Tomas suspected she had met one of the church's champions. Her gaze was down and locked on the floor. In time, she spoke again. "The worst thing is, I truly believed. Now I look back on it, and it was terrible, but the church tells us that all that is human is good, and hosts defied the Creator's blessings for a short, brutal life of killing. I didn't know any hosts personally, so it all seemed right."

Tomas pushed down his anger as deep as it would go.

Rachel was the worst villain he'd ever met, in large part because she hadn't even thought she was doing wrong. For all of Ghosthands's schemes, he, at least, had known the horror of what he did. If the knowledge locked in her mind wasn't so valuable, and if her life wasn't tied to that of Ben and Olena's, he wouldn't have hesitated to kill her where she sat, remorse or not.

"What changed your mind?" he forced himself to ask.

"Visiting the lab outside of Razin," she answered. She twirled her thumbs, never once looking up.

"We'd been receiving reports for years, so I knew well enough what was happening. But it's different, reading something on paper. When you read it, you can put distance between you and what's happening. You can convince yourself that maybe it's not all that bad and that what you're doing is right."

She shook her head but still didn't look up. "Then I visited and saw it with my own eyes. How they kept the kids locked in these tiny cages. The way they screamed when the inquisitors hurt them. I've never wanted kids. Don't really like them all that much, if I'm being true. But seeing that still hurt me, and it hurt me even more knowing that I'd ordered the tests."

When Rachel finally looked up, her eyes were rimmed with red. "I kept it together on that visit, but when I returned to my lab, I made plans to leave. As much as I wanted to know about the nexuses, I didn't want to be a part of that. I gathered together all the money I had, decided on a route and a destination, and left."

Tomas felt as though she was leaving substantial parts of her story out. "What about the murders you're wanted for?"

Rachel waved the question away. "I knew the church

wouldn't take kindly to my leaving, but I underestimated their reaction. As soon as I didn't report into work as expected, and they couldn't find me, they set up the murder charges. I don't even know the people they say I killed. But it closed down transportation options and unwittingly enlisted the marshals in the hunt for me. I had hoped to join a caravan heading west out of Razin, but one of Angela's marshals caught me before I could find one. And so here I am."

Tomas stood, unable to sit and listen any longer. It was interesting that Rachel was running away from the church, but he didn't think he was making the same connections that Angela was. He turned his next question on the marshal. "So, how does any of this matter?"

"She wants to get away from the church, and we want to keep her away from the church. We're allies here. She's said that she's willing to help us, if we'll help her."

Tomas looked between the women, half-formed plans baking in his mind. He turned to Rachel. "How far are you willing to go to help us out?"

Rachel nodded eagerly. "I'll do anything that will help me get away and start a new life."

Tomas didn't trust Rachel, but for what he was thinking, he didn't really need to. If the Family assassin killed her, Tomas wouldn't shed a single tear. He nodded to Angela. "Then let's get this assassin off our backs once and for all."

The preparations for the ambush took them most of the remaining time the assassin had left Tomas, although the ambush itself was as simple as he and Angela could imagine. What consumed most of their time was planning for and countering all the ways their plan could go wrong. First and most importantly, it meant protecting Olena, Ben, and the children under their care. Tomas also worried about Angela, but she was a marshal and accepted the dangers of her choices. What small wisdom Tomas possessed suggested silence, and he swallowed whatever objections he might have.

Their lack of knowledge complicated matters. It seemed as good as certain that the church was here with their knights, but neither Angela nor Tomas could guess at their number or location. Angela ordered one of her marshals to watch the mission while they prepared the ambush, but she reported back that she had seen nothing unusual. The Family was another question. Somehow, Tomas suspected the assassin he'd met wasn't working alone. He doubted the assassin had the dozen warriors he claimed, but the number was almost certainly more than zero.

All of which was to say, they didn't know who was being watched, nor who was watching them.

They solved the problems as they came. The marshals' partners wandered over to Ben and Olena's, passing on plans and information while pretending to volunteer with the children. Over the course of the next day, the children left the house in ones and twos to safe houses around Razin. From those homes, volunteers ferried them out to the farm where Tomas, Angela, and Rachel stayed.

There was something darkly ironic in summoning the children out to the very place that had once served as the gateway to hell for lost children. But Tomas hoped that the place that had once been their doom could now be their salvation. It was as an ideal location as one could get. The farmhouse had already been converted to house many people, and it was positioned on a small rise in the never-ending prairie that allowed a single rifle on the roof to watch for miles in any direction. Tomas still would have preferred thick walls and a unit of army snipers, but he could work with what they had.

Ben and Olena were the last to arrive, but Tomas barely had time to do more than accept their thanks and make sure they wanted nothing. There was much more that he and Ben needed to talk about, but he hoped to have that conversation tomorrow after he defeated the Family assassin.

By the time all was said and done, all of Angela's remaining marshals stood guard at the farmhouse while Angela, Tomas, and Rachel returned on horseback to Razin.

Angela had argued against this part of the plan. She felt safer having more rifles at her back, but Tomas had argued and won the point. If anything, he felt there weren't enough rifles at the farmhouse. That was the place he wanted protected more than anyplace else. Whatever happened in Razin, he and Angela would have to be enough. Besides, he was well aware of the average quality of the knights, and the Family assassin was perhaps one of the most dangerous hosts he had ever crossed blades with. As much as he hated bringing Angela with him, she was the best warrior among the marshals. Anyone else who came was likely to end up as a liability.

Everything about the location had been chosen carefully, and as simple as the plan was, there was still plenty that could go wrong. Near the edge of town, they dismounted from their horses and walked them to a hitching post where one of the marshals had promised to look over the horses while they prepared the ambush. From their dismount point, the walk to the meeting area was only four blocks. They were several hours early. Tolkin hadn't yet risen, and the night was as dark as it would ever be.

Tomas had sent his message to a local tavern with known Family associations, assuming the message would get to where it needed to go. The meeting was scheduled for when Tolkin was high in the sky, but if Tomas was the family assassin, he would come early and prepare his own ambush. The only way Tomas and Angela could think of beating the ambush was to arrive even earlier to set their own.

Angela left first to take up position, and the next few minutes were the worst for Tomas. He held his breath and strained his hearing for the sounds of either gunshots or a sword fight. He heard nothing that alarmed him, but he still had to resist the urge to follow Angela and ensure she had reached her sniper's nest without a problem.

To distract himself, he turned his attention to Rachel, who had curled up in the dark shadow of a house and was holding her knees close to her chest. She seemed nervous, but Tomas thought she was holding together remarkably well. "Don't worry. After tonight, I think the world is going to be quite a bit safer for you."

She shook her head. "Ever since I left, I haven't been sure that any place in the world will be safe for me."

"You had to realize that something like this was going to be in your future if you left. So why did you do it?"

Her angry glare surprised him. "Wouldn't you?"

Tomas shrugged. "Sure. But I'm a host and feel as human as I ever did. So, of course, I would do anything I could to distance myself from the church. But you believed in your work. Maybe you still do. From the way you told your story, I think you believe the life you were leading was a dream come true. So why give it all up? Why not swallow your discomfort and learn to live with it? I've met plenty of other believers who do."

Rachel's glare hardened. "I'm a scholar. When I learn something new that contradicts what I believe, I change my mind. I don't come up with strange justifications to defend my mistaken belief. Before I saw those children, I didn't think that what I was doing was evil. Now I do. I still hope to study the nexuses, but I'll find a better way."

Tomas let out a little grunt. "Not used to people changing their minds so easily. But if what you say is true, after tonight, hopefully, you'll be one step closer to finding a new way."

They lapsed into silence. Tomas kept his ears open and his senses sharp, but he noted nothing that gave him cause for concern. Razin went about its normal business, and the citizens went to sleep one by one. By the time Tolkin rose high in the sky, most of the city was asleep.

Remarkably, Rachel had dozed off too. Tomas jostled her awake. "Come on, it's time to go."

They slowly made their way from the edge of town to the intersection Tomas had decided on as their meeting place. Tomas took the lead, checking corners and watching rooftops for shadows that weren't supposed to move. Block by block, they advanced until they only had one turn to go to the intersection. Tomas poked his head out and saw that it was empty. That was good. He was still early and wanted to be first.

Elzeth lit in his stomach, and his senses grew sharper. He found the place where Angela had made her nest and watched her for several moments. She raised a hand that barely cleared the lip of the roof. If he hadn't known to look for it, he very much doubted he would have seen it. Her hand signs were quick and precise. Two snipers watched the intersection from down the street. Tomas took a deep breath and wished he could carry a stout iron door ahead of him as a shield. But if things went poorly, he'd have to settle for the scholar.

He turned back to Rachel. "Ready?"

She nodded quickly, and Tomas saw the first signs of her nerves. He reached into his pocket and pulled out a pair of manacles. She took a deep breath and held out her hands, and he fastened them. "Just remember, stay behind me until I tell you otherwise."

She nodded again.

Tomas took a deep breath of his own and then stepped out into the intersection. He walked a few feet down the street and waited. For some time, nothing happened, and Tomas couldn't even hear movement in any direction. Just as he was about to turn and call the whole deal off, a young man stepped from the shadows. Tomas's eyes narrowed.

The young man walked forward with all the unearned confidence of youth, a cocky swagger in his step. He spoke loudly enough that his voice carried down the street. "Boss has an alternative meeting place a few blocks that way." He stuck his finger out to the west.

They had expected something like this, and Tomas shook his head. Given the position of the Family snipers, it seemed reasonable to assume the assassin didn't think the gimmick would work. Although, it was also possible that the Family had enough rifles in town to cover several of the intersections. It didn't matter. He had Rachel, who was the one person every criminal in this damn town wanted. He called back. "No. If you want her, the trade happens here. I'm not walking into any ambush."

The kid grinned, clearly expecting the response. "Then

you hand her over to me, eh? Problem solved. My boss, he doesn't want to walk into any ambush either."

The young man took a step forward, and in the blink of an eye, Tomas had drawn his dagger and held it to Rachel's throat. He hadn't warned her it might come to this, so there was no trace of deception on her face as she gasped in sudden fear. Tomas made his voice as cold as ice. "Your boss comes here, or I walk, and he can clean up the corpse. I want to see him face to face when he tells me Ben and the kids are safe."

The kid held up his hands in surrender. The smile never left his face, which made Tomas worry he was playing directly into their hands. "Sure thing, sure thing. Let me go fetch him."

The young man disappeared around the corner, and Tomas shifted his position so that he stood behind Rachel. He kept the knife to her throat, and he could feel her heart pounding in her chest. This hadn't been what they talked about, but he didn't dare even whisper a reassurance, as a host might hear it. He kept using her as a shield while he watched for the snipers on the rooftop.

It took him a while. They were hidden almost as well as Angela, but they weren't as good at being still. Subtle motions caught his eye, and he soon knew where both were. Several minutes later, the assassin finally appeared. He stood out in the open, but his eyes searched the rooftops, just as Tomas had done.

Tomas forced himself to breathe evenly. He hated that everything relied on Angela, but they hadn't come up with a better plan. Any mistake might ruin the plan. They needed the assassin distracted, just for the moment Angela needed to aim and fire. It was the only way to guarantee a hit.

Tomas had hoped Angela would take the shot right

away, but the assassin's eyes never left the rooftops, even as he spoke. "I'm impressed. I didn't think you'd see reason so easily."

Tomas didn't move from behind Rachel. "I want your word that Ben, Olena, and the children will be safe."

The assassin still didn't let his eyes drop. Tomas had no doubt he was burning his sagani just as hot as Tomas was. A glint of moonlight off the barrel of Angela's rifle would be enough to give the ambush away.

The assassin answered. "Once I have the scholar, you have my word."

Tomas trusted that about as far as he could spit, so it wasn't hard to pretend he was skeptical. As soon as he let Rachel go, he'd also be exposed. His stomach clenched at the thought, but they still hadn't gotten Angela her shot. "Fine."

At his command, Elzeth burned even brighter, nearing unity. Tomas pushed Rachel forward. If she was looking to betray them, there'd never be a better time.

The assassin's attention remained on the rooftops.

When Rachel reached the assassin, everything happened at once.

The assassin raised a hand and gestured at Tomas. Rachel threw a cloud of sand in the assassin's face, then stepped to the side. Tomas shifted at the assassin's gesture, and both ends of the street erupted in gunfire.

Tomas's evasion caused one sniper to miss, but the other grazed his right arm. Fire burned up his shoulder, but he ignored it.

The assassin wasn't so lucky. Rachel's sand had caught him unawares, and for a moment, he was frozen. Angela used that moment to send a slug through his chest. Tomas saw blood spread across his shirt as his knees buckled under him.

Had it just been Tomas, he could have been in the alleys before the snipers launched their second volley. But Rachel had proven herself, so he had to keep her safe. She ran toward him, but he covered most of the distance. When they neared, Tomas looked over her shoulder and saw two more rifles emerge on the street a few blocks away.

He swore to himself. The Family had brought more help than Tomas had prepared for.

He pulled on Rachel's manacles and twirled around her so that he was between her and the rifles. Then he launched them both toward the nearest alley. He was almost fast enough. Two of the four rifles caught him on the next volley. One ripped through his side and the other through his left calf.

The sudden loss of strength in the leg caused him to fall, but he fell into the alley. Rachel didn't fall but stared at him in shock.

Tomas swore and pushed himself to his feet. He couldn't put much weight on the left leg, and once he let Elzeth rest, he knew he was in for a world of pain. But for now, he could hobble on it. He risked a glance back at the street.

The assassin lay still, blood pooling around his body. Tomas wanted to make sure he was dead, but the four rifles and his wounds prevented him. Another volley of shots tore up the corner of the house he used for cover and he ducked back into the alley. "We need to get back to the horses. Can you help me?"

Rachel nodded and took some of his weight. Together they hobbled back to the horses, where Angela waited for them with a concerned look. "Are you hurt?"

"Nothing that won't heal. But we need to get out of here," Tomas said.

They mounted the horses, and Tomas was grateful to have something carrying him away. They rode into the night, and Tomas wondered if he would ever see Razin again.

Right now, he was ready to put the damned city behind him for good.

15

Quinton was sleeping peacefully when the volleys of gunshots woke him. He was out of bed with his sword in hand in a moment, and he went to the window and looked out. More gunshots chased the first volley, giving him an idea of where in Razin the battle took place.

He briefly considered retrieving his remaining knights but decided against it. While he had little doubt they, too, would have been awakened by the fight, this seemed like a task easier completed on his own. To avoid questions from the innkeeper, he dropped out of his open window onto the street behind the inn. Another set of shots echoed across the quiet town, confirming the general location of Quinton's guess.

He didn't believe in coincidences. If there was a battle happening somewhere in town tonight, the odds were good that it had to do with Rachel. They'd been licking their wounds, but they'd been searching the town high and low for the scholar, who seemed like she'd up and vanished.

This was their first lead. He breathed in deeply and allowed the demon to ignite within him, and he ran like the wind before a summer storm.

Despite the size of Razin, it didn't take him long to approach the site of the shots. He slowed and walked cautiously, searching for signs of the fight. He heard rushing footsteps fleeing the scene, followed by the curses of two men swearing at one another. Quinton shifted his direction so he could intercept them. Two blocks later, they ran right in front of him with their rifles slung across their shoulders. They weren't any of the town's marshals, and they lacked the discipline of a knight. There was only one interested party that made any sense: the Family was here too.

That complicated matters, but it also gave Quinton a suspect for the first explosion outside the prison.

He let the two run. They didn't strike him as warriors worth his time. He went the way they had come from and found the site of the battle soon after. Quinton observed as much as he could from the corner of an alley. Given the casings littering the surrounding ground, he assumed this was where at least two of the rifles had been firing from. But at whom? He couldn't see any bodies on the street. He looked and listened for another few moments before stepping out into the intersection.

There, about a block away, was a life-threatening puddle of blood. He advanced towards that. Most of the blood was still wet and fresh, and it looked like enough had been spilled to kill a man. Yet there was no corpse.

Quinton stood up from his examination and studied the surrounding area. It was difficult to tell, but it didn't look like a corpse had been dragged away. But to the north, he found a trail of blood. He scratched at his chin and followed it.

If someone had lost that amount of blood and lived to tell the tale, Quinton would have put money on them being a host, a complication he didn't need. This mission was going to be difficult enough with just Tomas standing in the way.

He kept one hand on the hilt of his sword. Initially, the trail was marked by thick, infrequent pools, but it didn't take long for them to become few and far between. Either the victim had lost all their blood, or their wounds were healing. And Quinton was pretty sure which one he would guess. He was on the trail of another damned demon. Razin seemed like it was crawling with them.

The trail stopped in the middle of a residential district. Quinton made a small circle, searching for tracks, but found nothing conclusive.

His sagani-enhanced hearing picked up a stifled groan a little further north.

No coincidences.

Quinton followed the sound, and when he turned a corner, he finally found the demon he'd been tracking.

All of his guesses were confirmed with a quick glance. The tattoos marked the man as a member of the Family, and the bloody hole in his shirt spoke to the trauma he'd just endured. He looked to be small, though it was hard to tell with his knees tucked tightly against his chest. His hair was so light that it reflected Tolkin's light like a freshly whitewashed fence.

He looked like a wounded animal, but Quinton wasn't so sure. The man was tired, exhausted, and bloody, but Quinton couldn't see any actual wounds on his skin. The man's breathing was quick but not labored in the way Quinton would expect if his organs were failing. Quinton stopped several paces away, wary.

The man offered a sardonic smile. "Ghosthands. I didn't think the church would send you. Although I suppose it makes sense. Are you here for Tomas or the woman?"

Quinton was aware of the moniker he'd earned based on his sword technique. He found it annoying but ignored that for now. "For the scholar, killing Tomas is simply an unexpected side benefit."

"I'm surprised he survived your first meeting. I've crossed swords with him, and I have to confess that I wasn't impressed."

Quinton usually believed himself to be above insults, but the Family swordsman was deliberately provoking him. The blonde man wanted him to attack. "From where I'm standing, it doesn't look like your encounter went much better."

The man chuckled and nodded. Quinton noted that the laughter came easily. Despite the amount of blood this man had lost, Quinton suspected he was nearly healed. "You've got a point there," the Family swordsman said.

"I don't suppose you're going to tell me why the Family is interested in the scholar."

"No big secret. She's got the plans for a weapon that will change the course of history knocking around in her head. We want it. Lacking that, we want to make sure nobody else gets it."

Quinton appreciated the blunt honesty, but it only made him more certain that this wounded animal pose was little more than a trap. His blood sang in his veins at the thought. This man was a host and deserved nothing but a slow, painful death. Quinton would be delighted to offer it to him.

The smile hadn't left the warrior's face. "I don't suppose you'd be interested in teaming up, would you? That army unit is scheduled to arrive tomorrow. And I'll confess, I'm not sure I have enough guns to get through that. We could work together and then fight each other after Tomas, the marshals, and the army are all dead."

Quinton actually almost considered it. The man's plain speaking was almost enough to sway him. But not quite. He was an unnecessary complication. "Or you could get up, and we could fight now and be done with it."

"But I'm wounded." A sly smile gave the half-hearted attempt at deception away.

When Quinton didn't budge, the man grinned wider. "I suppose you got me. Thought I could fool you. But I suppose your reputation is deserved. Hopefully, you're a better fight than Tomas. I would have killed him easily in a duel."

Quinton drew his sword. "I can guarantee that I am."

The assassin rose smoothly to his feet and drew his daggers. "Bold words. Let's see if you can back them up."

The assassin leaped forward with a speed Quinton almost didn't believe was possible. Even though he'd been ready for the attack, it was all he could do to stay away from the deadly blade. The tip of a man's sword flicked out like a snake's tongue, cutting at limbs and arteries in no particular pattern.

The demon within Quinton blazed, and he met the assault as well as he could. The Family assassin had a slight edge in speed, but Quinton's technique was just a hair better, leaving them as evenly matched as any opponent Quinton had ever fought.

After another exchange, the assassin broke apart, and the smile on his face was wider than ever. "I'm impressed. I don't think I've ever crossed swords with anyone like you."

Quinton's heart pounded in his ears, and it took him a moment to identify the feeling that consumed him. It was joy. Here, at last, he had finally found an opponent truly worthy of his skill. An opponent who, he had to admit, was as likely to kill him as the other way around. It was a glorious experience and worth treasuring. "That skill doesn't just come from a sagani. Where did you learn?"

"The First Squad, First Army, at your service."

The best of the best. And that was before he'd become a host. No wonder he was a worthy opponent. Quinton offered the barest hint of a bow. "It is a pleasure to finally cross swords with someone worthy."

The assassin's smile said that he agreed. "Likewise." They met again at the small intersection in this frontier town in the middle of nowhere, and it was everything Quinton dreamed of. Both warriors opened up wounds on the other, but neither could gain a decisive advantage. They passed and passed again, leaving their blood and sweat on the streets.

The pounding of feet behind them caused the combatants to break away. Quinton turned to see his knights, who should have stayed behind, at the end of the street, rushing to his aid.

The assassin saw them coming and dipped his head toward Quinton. "Until we meet again." And then he disappeared around the corner, running faster than Quinton could follow. Quinton gave a step to follow, but his knees wobbled and he stopped. He took a deep breath and looked down at himself, covered in cuts from head to toe. None were fatal, but more than a few were as close as he'd come to a killing blow in a long time.

He swore and slammed his sword back into his sheath.

What he wanted was to resume this fight, but the knights reminded him that his duty was to find a scholar and bring her to safety.

Once the job was done, he could have all the fun he wanted.

16

After the chaos of the last few days, the rendezvous with the army was delightfully straightforward. Angela had sent a messenger to meet the approaching unit and give them directions to the farmhouse. After killing the Family assassin, they'd returned to the farmhouse and slept for the rest of the night. By the time they woke, the army was already near.

Tomas sat with Ben on the porch. The sounds of children running, arguing, and preparing for the day served as a constant backdrop. The front door opened, and Angela and Rachel stepped through. Until the door closed, the porch was twice as loud as it had been, rendering conversation impossible. The door closed on a chorus of groans. No small number of the children wanted to join Angela and meet with the soldiers.

"Let's go," Angela said.

"If you don't mind, I'm going to stay here," Tomas said.

"Why?"

"I want to talk to Ben before we leave."

Angela shook her head. "I'm sure the commander is going to want to meet you."

"And we'll have plenty of time between here and Porum. This is more important."

It looked like she was about to fight him over it, but then she shrugged. "Suit yourself, I suppose." She and Rachel stepped off the porch and walked to where the unit had stopped. Tomas watched them for a bit, using the distraction as a way to delay saying what needed to be said. Ben, for his part, seemed perfectly content to sit and watch the world go by.

"I'm sorry about what I said last time," Tomas said.

"You're forgiven."

"That simple?"

"That simple."

Tomas scratched at his chin. "I've been thinking a lot about what you said. Do you truly believe the church doesn't need to be destroyed?"

"I think these plans to build super-weapons need to be stopped, and I care little for the knights, inquisitors, and champions, but I don't think the church needs to fall completely. It needs to change."

"Sometimes it's easier to change when everything burns down and you start from scratch."

"True enough, but the scale of the church is incredible. There's a reason the army hasn't shut down the churches in the east, even as they fight the church for land out west. It's a part of society, and one we need. Burning it down would hurt tens of thousands, if not hundreds of thousands, of people."

"So, what do you think I should do?"

"Mostly what you're doing now. Stop them from developing that weapon. After that, rest. You're only one man, and not even you can bring down the church. Accept that you've carried your burden far enough and lay it down before you drag it through the gate with you."

Tomas chewed on that as he watched Angela speaking with the commander of the unit. He was a young man, clean-shaven, with a rifle across his back and a belt of ammunition around his waist. He looked like a child. Perhaps Ben had a point. Perhaps he was getting too old for this.

Though it was the discussion of the church that had angered Tomas the most last time, those weren't the words that had lingered longest in his memory. "When we spoke last, you said that I needed to search myself for the peace I was lacking. I've thought about that since then, too, and I have to admit that I don't think I know how."

Ben smiled widely. "You're a remarkable person, Tomas. Few would ask that question. To fight the war raging inside of you, the answer is simple. You need to understand yourself."

"I'd say after all these years stuck with myself, I have a pretty good idea of what I'm like."

Ben's smile didn't fade. "I know it seems easy, but it's anything but. I've been working on trying to understand myself for the last two decades, and I'm still not sure I've found the total truth about who I am. You can tell me if I'm wrong, but I imagine it will be even harder for you as you share your mind with Elzeth. You'll have to separate what is you and what is sagani, and after all these years, that's a monumental task."

Tomas shifted in his chair. "I don't mean any disrespect, but I don't think I believe you. I know who I am."

"Why do you fight, Tomas? You told me that for years,

your only thought was to head out west and put your past behind you. So why haven't you done that?"

"I am going to go out west, just as soon as I stop the church from developing the super-weapon."

Ben shook his head. "You're lying to yourself."

Tomas clenched his fist, but he held onto his temper. "What do you mean?"

"It's not like going out west is hard for someone like you. You literally just turn toward the sunset and keep walking. If that was truly what you wanted, more than anything else, you'd be far beyond the reach of the church already. Perhaps you'd be in an unexplored land that has never seen a human footprint. But you keep coming back, and yes, your reasons always sound good, but I'm asking you to ask yourself why. Why do you really keep coming back? Is it because you need to feel needed? Or do you want to fight for a reason bigger than yourself? I don't know the answer, but I don't think you do either. So tell me I'm wrong. Tell me: *Why do you fight?*"

The sincerity behind the question broke past Tomas's defenses. A dozen answers came to mind, but as he considered them, he realized none was quite true. None explained why he hadn't just kept walking west. Had he lied to himself all this time? "I don't know," he admitted.

Ben seemed pleased by the answer. "That's what I mean by understanding. Once you understand yourself, you'll be on the road to peace."

"You think I can find it in the time I have left?"

"No idea. But it's a journey worth taking. Trust me on that. It's changed my life."

Out in the fields, Angela and the commander looked like they were finishing their discussion. Tomas stood. "I'm sorry my arrival brought more chaos into your life."

Ben laughed. "Tomas, I have no less than a dozen kids

hanging around my house all day, every day. Trust me, you're not adding that much chaos. In fact, Olena and I were just saying that we kind of like this farmhouse. There's a lot more space out here. We might have to convince the marshals to sell it to us."

"I'm sure Angela would give you a pretty good deal on the place," Tomas said.

"I'm sure. You take care of her. She might not say it, but your leaving hit her pretty hard. She was moping for a long time after. I know you two haven't figured everything out yet, but she's worth fighting for, too."

"You'll hear no argument from me there," Tomas said.

"Good."

"You take care of yourself, too. I imagine once we're gone, the danger will be past, but keep those daggers of yours close to hand."

"I always do," Ben said.

They parted that day as friends, which Tomas was grateful for. He had a feeling he'd never see the old inquisitor again.

Tomas, Angela, and Rachel joined the army unit with little fuss. The commander was named Seth, and he went about the work of escorting them with a precision that would have made the most demanding of generals proud. The unit traveled with three covered wagons that were kept spaced apart and buttoned up, preventing any hopeful assassin with a rifle from spotting Rachel and putting a bullet in her from far away.

Seth's soldiers took their task seriously, too. About a third were on duty at any time, riding in a loose circle around the wagons. They kept their eyes focused outward and their rifles close.

Tomas had offered his services to Seth as soon as he'd finished speaking with Ben, and Seth had been welcoming enough, but he'd also made it clear there was little need for Tomas. His soldiers had served together for years and knew how to fight together. Tomas settled for promising Seth that he'd be ready if ever the need arose.

The travel left Tomas in the unusual position of not having many responsibilities. If he'd wanted, he could have curled up in one of the wagons and fallen asleep as the horses pulled him toward Porum.

He didn't, though he couldn't deny the temptation. He still couldn't discern any certain signs of madness, but if he was nearing the end of his days, he didn't want to spend them sleeping in a hot wagon. Far better to appreciate the endless expanse of the frontier.

One night, about halfway through their journey, Angela left the circled wagons and wandered some distance away. Tomas watched her go but didn't follow. They'd been cordial the entire trip but nothing more. He'd caught her watching him frequently, but every time he did, she simply looked away.

"You should go talk to her," Elzeth said.

"What if she doesn't want me to?"

"Then she'll tell you. She's not exactly one to hold back."

Fortified with Elzeth's courage, he left the circled wagons and followed her trail. When he reached her, he asked, "Mind if I join you?"

"Not at all."

He sat down next to her, feeling as though he'd already won a small victory. She was looking up at the stars, and he tilted his head up so he could also enjoy the view. "I feel like I owe you an apology," he said.

"What for?"

"For bringing as much trouble into your life as I did. And, maybe, for leaving."

"You don't sound so sure about the leaving part."

Her tone was flat, and Tomas couldn't decide if it was because she was angry or because she was trying to hide some other emotion from him. "I didn't want to ruin your life by forcing you to join me on the run. What I didn't count on was that when I left you, I ruined my life."

"And now, what? You come back here thinking that maybe we can pick up where we left off?"

"The thought had crossed my mind."

"But you're only going to leave again. You said it yourself when we spoke back in Razin. Madness is just around the corner. So why should I let myself care when I know you won't be around for much longer?"

He was ashamed to admit the thought hadn't occurred to him. He'd focused much more on the time remaining than on what her life would be like after he was gone.

Tomas swallowed hard. "And now I feel like I owe you another apology. I keep thinking about myself and the time I have left, and what I want to do with that time. All I could think about was spending as much of it with you as I could. But I didn't think through what all that meant to you. I'm sorry."

Angela sighed. "I get why you left, and as much as it hurt, I understood. I still think your heart is in the right place, but I can't just pick up like nothing has happened. And I don't think I want to try, knowing what's coming. Fair?"

Tomas's heart felt like a piece of wood split open by an axe, but he nodded. "Of course."

He made to leave, but Angela stopped him. "You don't need to go anywhere. It's still good to see you, and I'm glad you're here. We don't need to be strangers."

Her words were a balm to his broken heart, and he settled back into the grass to join her in watching the stars.

17

Tomas, Angela, and Seth left the wagons behind to scout Porum. The wagons had stopped at Tomas's request, though Tomas suspected Seth was humoring him more than respecting his opinion. The wagons were a mile back, circled around a small knoll.

They stopped about a half mile from the outskirts of the town. Tomas and Seth each produced a looking glass and took turns sharing with Angela.

Tomas saw a dying town, grasping out for a future that Razin had stolen. Like almost all frontier towns, most of the buildings looked like they'd been raised within the last five years. But unlike most frontier towns, many of the buildings were nothing more than hollowed-out shells. Windows were dark and boarded up, and weeds overgrew the gardens.

It was painful to see, like watching a wounded soldier suffer in agony before they died from blood loss.

Angela had shared the details of Porum's slow death. The Great West Railroad Company had chosen Porum as the endpoint of their enormous rail line. Like Razin, it had been an active trading post in its earliest years, and when the announcement of the railroad landed, it pulled settlers to the small settlement like a magnet attracts iron.

The Great Western Railroad Company spent through their coffers too fast, and a pair of costly engineering mistakes had slowed their progress considerably. Their biggest competitor, the Northern Transport Company, had smelled blood and moved in for the kill. They declared the construction of their own line, originating closer to the bigger cities in the northeast corner of the country and ending in Razin. They built slowly but steadily, eventually overtaking the Great Western.

Traders had no problem predicting the future, and Razin became the largest magnet in the area, drawing prospective businesses away from Porum.

Eventually, a new owner bought out the Great Western Railroad Company and hurried to finish the railroad line, but it was too late. Businesses didn't trust the word of the company, and the Northern Transport Company's line passed through more populated cities. The Great Western Railroad Company teetered on the brink of collapse, owners of a railroad line nobody wanted to use.

Though the giant companies had fought most of their battles in the markets out east, Porum was the greatest casualty of their clash. For a handful of years, it had been one of the most coveted destinations in the west, and its growth had reflected that desire. But no longer. Hopeful settlers abandoned their new homes, pulling up their roots once again to chase the slim hope of a better life somewhere else.

All of which made it a very unfortunate place to be escorting the most wanted person in the west through. A crowded city like Razin meant witnesses on every corner and crowds to blend into. An abandoned city like Porum meant ample places for assassins to hide.

"Looks quiet to me," Seth said.

"Too quiet?" Tomas asked Angela.

She grunted as she peered through Seth's looking glass. "I can't say I'm the best person to ask. It's been over a year since I've visited, and even that was only for a day. It was quiet then, too."

"Do you think that maybe you're overreacting?" Seth asked Tomas.

"If it was me up against you, Porum is where I'd set up. Out in the prairie, you can see for miles, and those rifles reach a lot longer than my sword. And you lead them well. Any attack would have been nearly impossible."

Tomas paused and gestured toward the town. "But down there? I can hide. I can get close enough that your rifles aren't as dangerous."

Angela snorted. "Tell that to the Family assassin."

Tomas ignored the comment. "Not only that, but we're up against the church, and I'd be willing to bet the church has believers in Porum willing to help. It's a town that has fallen upon hard times, and hard times are fertile ground for the church's missionaries. I can't say for sure that they're waiting for us down there, but it's not worth taking the risk."

Seth didn't dismiss Tomas's concerns. "What would you recommend?"

Tomas had been considering that question for some time. "There aren't many good options. My best suggestion is to wait until about an hour before the train is due to leave. Then we charge into town and get onto the train."

"Why not just go commandeer one of those empty

houses now, so we don't have to fight our way through town tomorrow?"

"If I'm right, you're going to have to fight your way through town one way or the other. Better to only have to do it once. Besides, I trust your soldiers and your rifles more out here than I do in the city."

Seth chewed on his lower lip. "Hard to believe one scholar is worth all this trouble. Could have done without the lot of them growing up, if you ask me."

"I've experienced the results of her line of research firsthand outside of Kimson," Tomas reminded Seth. "It makes cannons look like children's playthings."

Seth spit. "Fair enough. I don't like it, but better to play it safe than pay for being overconfident. We stay out here tonight, and tomorrow we ride into Porum. But I'm telling the soldiers it's your fault we can't stay at an inn tonight."

After supper that night, Tomas left the rest of the unit behind. There'd been no sign of an attack, but Seth was doubling the watch tonight to be safe. The army commander wasn't interested in becoming friends, but Tomas respected a leader who listened to suggestions and changed their mind. In his experience, most leaders were more prone to doubling down on their mistakes. He appreciated not having to fight allies and enemies.

He found a quiet place to sit. Clouds had moved in after the sun had set, so there wasn't much in the way of stars, but he could see the faint outline of Tolkin when the clouds thinned. Tomas reached his hand into his pocket and pulled out the small nexus. It was still wrapped in a handkerchief, and he'd gotten used to its quiet but ever-present song over the months. Tonight he unveiled it, staring at the pale blue light it emitted.

He'd tried asking Rachel about her work, but she'd made it clear that she felt more comfortable keeping the secrets of the nexuses to herself.

Tomas supposed he couldn't blame her after everything the church had done, but the lack of knowledge irritated him.

"What's bothering you?" Elzeth asked.

The sagani's voice actually startled him. They hadn't been speaking much lately, and Elzeth had seemed more lethargic than usual. On their ride over, it wasn't unusual for Tomas to go most of the day without feeling Elzeth's presence.

"What's not bothering me?" he asked bitterly. "Things haven't worked out with Angela. I'm convinced a small army of knights is waiting for us in Porum, and I don't know what's happening to us or how long we have."

To prove his point, he held out his empty left hand. "It's still perfectly steady. Always has been. If we're going mad, where are the tics?"

"None of that's what's really bothering you, though."

Tomas almost asked how Elzeth could be so sure, but he held his tongue. Elzeth could feel the emotions coursing through him. It made it nearly impossible to lie to the sagani.

"It feels like I'm quickly running toward enemies I can't beat, and I don't know why the hell I'm even running in this direction."

Elzeth stirred in Tomas's stomach. "This is about what Ben said?"

"Yeah, I think so."

"What's got you so worked up about it?"

"I think he's right. As it is, I'm going to keep running around, chasing after everything that grabs my attention until I'm nothing more than a madman. What I'm doing isn't working, Elzeth. I'm not any closer to feeling a sense of peace than when I first stepped into Razin. If anything, I'm further away."

Elzeth pondered the question silently, but Tomas felt the sagani's mixed feelings as he stirred within Tomas's core. Finally, Elzeth said, "What do you mean when you say that you want to live in peace? Is it just that you don't want to fight, or is there something more than that?"

"Something more." Tomas struggled to find the appropriate description. "I want to feel like I've atoned for my sins."

"Do you think that there's something you can do, some action you can complete, that will help you feel that way? I'm doubtful."

"Me too. But if there's nothing I do that helps, why am I fighting?"

"I've been wondering the same about me," Elzeth admitted.

"Really?"

"What we saw in Kimson, I'm still trying to wrap my thoughts around it. More memories have returned, but not enough that makes sense. Why have I jumped from host to host, and what's different with you? I've been thinking about these questions non-stop since then, and I'm driving myself mad with a lack of answers."

"Is that why you've been so quiet lately?"

"One of the big reasons. But the more I think about it, the more I realize how much it doesn't matter."

Tomas was surprised. Elzeth spoke with impressive conviction. "How so?"

"Human imagination and thoughts are wonderful gifts, but they carry a burden most animals never have to worry about. You keep trying to plan and predict; you seek purpose in a purposeless world. It gives you strength and lets you build these towns across the frontier, but it denies you peace. It is, I think, one reason so many flock to the church. The teachings of the Creator give people purpose and a community to share that purpose with."

"You think I should join the church?"

"I'm not sure they'd welcome you as a new member, given your rocky history. What I'm saying is that maybe it's time for you to learn from the sagani. When we're unified, thought falls away and all that exists is this moment. Obviously, we should avoid actual unity as much as possible, but there's no reason you can't seek that same sort of mental peace. What we did in the past is in the past, and you can't change the future nearly as much as you think you can. So why not act in the best way you know how and let the world take care of the rest?"

Tomas grunted. "I think that's just about the longest monologue you've ever given."

"It's something that's been on my mind, too. The only way I know how to deal with it is by focusing on what's right in front of me. You're with Angela again, and if you can board that train tomorrow, you'll be robbing the church of one of its most powerful weapons. It seems to me you're right where you need to be."

Tomas hated to admit that the sagani's lecture had helped, but he felt more at ease than before.

"Thanks, old friend. Whatever happens tomorrow, I'm glad we get to suffer through it together."

"Until the end, Tomas."

"Until the end."

Tomas stood up and returned to the rest of the camp. Seth didn't have him on watch tonight, and he intended to get as much sleep as he could steal.

He had a train to catch tomorrow, and he wanted to be well-rested.

18

The sun rose in the east, but it barely did anything except make the overhanging clouds a little brighter than before. The air was thick with moisture, and the wind was picking up from the west. Tomas glanced in that direction; the sky was as dark as night. The storm looked to be heading straight for them. The only unanswered question was when it would hit.

Behind him, Angela and Seth argued about when they should leave for the station. Seth wanted to depart earlier to leave more time to find solutions if problems arose. Angela believed they should leave at the last possible moment. Either way, the train wouldn't wait for them. Not even an army could get the railroad companies to abandon their dedication to their precious timetables. When they couldn't settle the argument, they turned to Tomas.

"We should leave sooner rather than later. If I'm right and they're waiting for us, we're not going to want to miss our window, and we can't assume we'll be able to ride past them," he said.

Angela scowled. Her argument had been that the less

time they spent in Porum, the better. As far as the argument went, Tomas agreed, but it underestimated their opponents. With a proper ambush, it wouldn't be hard to delay the army escort long enough to miss their train. After a moment's consideration, she nodded. "Very well. We give everybody a chance to check their gear, then head out?"

Seth agreed and passed along the orders to his squad leaders. The camp was already mostly down, and now the soldiers finished the task. Once the packing was done, the soldiers checked their weapons and ammunition. Tomas took a glance at his own sword, but he always kept it ready for battle, so there was little to do.

Angela joined him as he sheathed his blade. "Be safe out there today."

Tomas grunted. "Not sure there's going to be anyplace safe in that town today, but I don't plan on dying."

She was about to leave when he stood and blocked her exit.

"That being said, I'm not sure what the day is going to bring. I'm going to say this now so I don't regret it if I don't get another chance. I carry a lot of regrets, but none bother me as much as the future we didn't get to have. Can't take back what happened, but there are many days I wish I could."

Angela swallowed, and she nodded. "Not always sure where I sit on such things, but there's been plenty of days when I've felt the same."

It wasn't quite the response Tomas hoped he'd get, but he understood her hesitation well enough. Why fall in love with a man who was likely to go mad within the year? If their positions were reversed, he'd be hesitant, too.

"Good luck," he said.

"You, too."

The rest of the escort was still finishing their preparations, so Tomas went over to where Rachel was sitting by herself. "How you feeling?"

"Nervous," she admitted.

"Nothing wrong with that. But we'll have you on that train when it leaves this morning, and you'll be able to start a new life."

Rachel nodded. "Thanks for all you've done. I'm grateful."

"Anytime, ma'am."

Seth shouted the order to mount up, and Tomas helped Rachel into the first of the covered wagons before sealing it up. He wished they had a stronger wagon with thick wooden walls, like the one the knights had built to transport him outside of Chesterton. Once the bullets started flying, and he was sure they would, the canvas of the wagon would be precious little protection.

"If the shooting starts, lay down as low as you can," he said.

Tomas mounted his horse, and they began their ride. To the west, fingers of lightning flickered down from the darkness to strike the prairie. The wind gusted, blowing dirt around and reducing the visibility. Tomas supposed that would be a good thing. The less distance the rifles could reach, the safer they were.

Seth set a hard pace, pushing the covered wagons nearly as fast as they could go over the old, rutted track that served as the path between Razin and Porum. The wagons jostled and shook, and Tomas was grateful to be on the horse.

They covered the remaining distance to Porum in less than an hour, and soon they passed the location they'd scouted from the day before. Seth sent a pair of scouts up ahead to examine their route through town. He planned on following the road, which met up with one of the major streets in Porum and led straight to the station in the center of the town. The route had the advantage of simplicity, and it would permit the covered wagons without problem, but it was also the most obvious route potential ambushers would stake out.

They were well within a half-mile of Porum when Seth called a halt to the advance. The scouts had disappeared into town but had yet to reappear. By Tomas's own mental math, they should have reported some time ago. No one had heard any rifles, but there were a lot of ways to kill a soldier, and no small number of them were silent. A sinking certainty grew in Tomas's stomach. Danger lurked within Porum's innocent-looking homes and businesses, and they had little choice but to walk straight into it.

Seth called for him and Angela, and his sentences were clipped and terse. "Options?"

"We need to assume that the scouts are down. We could send more in after them, but I fear we'd only be helping our enemies thin our numbers," Angela said.

"I hate the idea of waltzing in without knowing what we're in for," Seth argued.

Tomas sighed. "I'll go on ahead. Give me a half hour. If you haven't seen or heard from me by then, you might as well all come charging. And if you hear rifles, I wouldn't mind some support."

"You think you can just ride in there?" Seth asked.

"I'm going to ride around and approach from the west. I suspect the ambushers are focused east, especially now that we're in view."

The low rumble of thunder echoed in the distance. The storm was catching up quickly. Seth considered for a moment, then nodded. "Good luck."

Without further ado, Tomas broke away from the rest of the group and galloped his horse north and west. He circled so that he kept plenty of distance between him and Porum, but he pushed his horse as hard as it would go. When he felt as though he was relatively safe, he took a deep breath and turned the horse toward the town. He pressed himself against the horse's back, ignoring the pain of the poor riding posture.

No bullets reached out for him, and he slowed the horse as soon as he was within the town. He leaped off and proceeded deeper on foot.

Now that he was closer, the problems Porum faced were even more clear. They had boarded windows up as hopeful citizens gave up on their dreams and left. Paint peeled on buildings that still looked new. The street Tomas was on was quiet. Not the quiet that came from families enjoying a meal at home together, but the quiet that came from abandoned homes and dreams. Tomas had heard stories of ghost towns throughout the west, built on a sliver of a prayer and abandoned when reality sank its teeth down to the bone. He'd never visited one, though this part of Porum gave him a sense of what one might feel like.

He kept his eyes open for movement, both in the darkened windows and along the rooftops. As near as he could tell, the only living things within several blocks were him and the horse he'd ridden in on. He advanced cautiously but quickly. At each corner, he poked his head around, exposing himself to new lines of sight. As he approached the center of town, it started to feel less abandoned. The houses here were in slightly better repair. A few had windows open, but no one was out in the streets.

There was no reason for the town to be so quiet. With a train departing today, it stood to reason that local store owners would be tripping over themselves to pack and ship their goods. Travelers would be preparing to leave and kissing their families goodbye. Even in a town this small, there should have been more activity.

He chose the train station as his first destination. If there was anything wrong with the train, everything else was for naught. There was also a slight chance he could avoid confrontation if the ambushers were holed up on the east side of town. It was a hope, at least.

As soon as he had the thought, he worried he had doomed himself. Sure enough, just a few steps later, a figure strode into the intersection ahead of him. Tomas blinked at the familiar face, not quite believing what he was seeing. Of all the people he'd expected to come across, one hadn't even occurred to him. But now he was here, very much in the flesh.

Ghosthands stood before him, a wicked grin on his face.

"Hello, Tomas. It's been a long time."

19

Tomas glanced back the way he'd come, and he wasn't ashamed to admit the idea of turning tail seemed wisest. If he'd been confident that he could successfully flee, he would have in a moment. But Ghosthands's speed was likely superior to his own. He reached into his pocket and unwrapped the small nexus within, careful not to touch it. "I thought maybe you'd forgotten about me," he said.

Ghosthands's smile twitched so fast Tomas first thought it was a tic. It took him a moment to understand that he'd touched a nerve. Ghosthands admitted as much when he said, "To the contrary, my failure to kill you outside of Chesterton has become one of my greatest regrets."

"I'd say I'm sorry, but I'm not much for lying."

Ghosthands slowly and deliberately drew his sword. "It's time to finish this."

Tomas drew his own sword one-handed as Ghosthands settled into his stance.

"There's no point in fighting with anything less than unity," Tomas told Elzeth.

The sagani spun in circles around Tomas's core. For a

moment, Tomas feared Elzeth might refuse, but then he settled. "Doesn't mean I have to like it," he said.

Despite his complaint, Elzeth didn't resist when Tomas pulled down the thin veil that separated him and the sagani. As he did, he grabbed hold of the nexus and pressed it between his hand and the hilt of his sword. It sang to him, pulling his attention toward it. He opened himself up to the power of the nexus as the last shred of separation between him and Elzeth burned away. Power ripped through his body and sought to tear him apart.

He'd been through the transition often enough that he knew not to fight. Surviving the nexus was more about surrender than strength. He relaxed against the pain and let the power fill his limbs and sharpen his senses. Lines of power overlaid his vision, and Ghosthands grew almost as bright as the sun when he charged.

Unlike their first encounter, Ghosthands wasted no time teasing out Tomas's strength. They knew one another's abilities. Tomas took solace in knowing that Porum wouldn't be like Chesterton, where Ghosthands had sought to turn Tomas into the villain. Here, his only thought was to kill Tomas quickly.

Tomas was prepared. He brought up his sword, and the clash of steel sounded like a thunderclap to Tomas's sensitive ears. Ghosthands didn't relent. He tried to push Tomas's blade out of the way, muscles straining with the effort. When Tomas didn't budge, Ghosthands snapped his blade, using Tomas's sword as a fulcrum. Tomas slid back and dropped his sword low. He cut up at Ghosthands's wrists, but Ghosthands took a step back and parried the strike with ease.

Ghosthands didn't separate but stepped forward again, his spacing closer than Tomas expected. Tomas deflected most of the cut, but Ghosthands's blade scratched a line across his left shoulder.

It was a slight cut, but an unexpected surge of fury and fear exploded in Tomas's chest. He launched himself at Ghosthands, who wasn't prepared for either the strength or speed of the assault. Tomas scored two gashes against his enemy. One was across his chest, close to his heart, and the other was near the elbow. Both started to heal, but Tomas continued to press.

Unity had never been like this before. He was used to fighting on instinct and muscle memory, but emotion had never consumed him this way. He attacked and attacked, abandoning technique for the ever-increasing strength and speed unity promised. Ghosthands was retreating. Tomas's relentless assault left him no time to respond. His eyes widened, which only fed fuel to the fire consuming Tomas from the inside.

He was so close! Ghosthands's parries were coming later and later. Tomas was about to break Ghosthands's guard when he heard soft footsteps running at him from the south. He pressed his attack, but Ghosthands barely kept his sword between Tomas's blade and his heart. The footsteps grew closer, and Tomas had no choice but to disengage.

He wasn't a moment too soon. A long dagger passed less than the width of a hand in front of his face, and Tomas cut at the blonde-haired Family assassin. The assassin blocked the cut with his second dagger, but the force of Tomas's cut knocked the weapon from the assassin's hand. He skidded to a stop between Tomas and Ghosthands. Tomas retreated a few steps as Ghosthands regained his balance and took his position beside the assassin. The fear grew in his chest. This man was supposed to be dead.

"You two thought you could play without me? I'm hurt,"

the assassin said. Far from being bothered by the lack of a dagger, he reached behind him and pulled out another. He seemed remarkably healthy for a dead man.

"What are you doing here?" Ghosthands growled.

"Same thing you are. But I decided it was best for both of us if I helped you."

"Why?" asked Ghosthands.

"Because I'm not sure I can beat whatever he is right now. He's stronger than the last time I fought him. I figured we could take him out together; then I'll kill *you*."

Ghosthands eyed the assassin, then shrugged. "Fair enough." He nodded, and they came at Tomas together.

Tomas roared and met their charge with one of his own. They cut at him, but their blades were never quite fast enough. His instincts were sharper than his sword. Their bodies betrayed them, letting Tomas know where they would cut before their weapons began their deadly arcs. He felt like a sparrow among a pair of cows, flitting in between their cuts and striking before they could respond. He was light, carried by currents of power that were invisible to anyone besides him.

It was the freest he'd ever felt since the day he first signed up for the army, the day he felt he'd escaped the sword school to see the rest of the world. No one could touch him.

Until they could. He missed a step, and the Family assassin cut close to the back of Tomas's wrist. He was too slow on a parry, and Ghosthands cut near his elbow. They were both shallow cuts, more scratches than true wounds, but they punctured his sense of freedom like a bullet exploding a potato.

His answer was an attack that drove both Ghosthands and the Family assassin back. Tomas's wounds were already healed, and he fought like a cornered animal. His sword sliced through the muscle of the assassin's chest. When Ghosthands tried to help defend his new ally, Tomas lashed out, snaking through Ghosthands's guard and stabbing him. Ghosthands took the blade in the shoulder and stumbled back.

As soon as he won a sliver of space, he bolted away from the others. The assassin stumbled onto his feet but was too slow to catch Tomas. Tomas sprinted around the corner, climbed up the wall of an abandoned house like a spider, and pressed himself against the roof.

His heart pounded in his chest, like an explosion of dynamite going off within him a dozen times for every breath. His body trembled, and he laid the sword gently down beside him. The nexus filled him with a sweet power and a promise of oblivion. It was embedded in his palm and warm to the touch. With his right hand, Tomas pried the stone from his palm. His left grabbed the handkerchief, wrapped the stone within, and returned it to his left pocket.

With the nexus handled, Tomas tried to replace the wall between him and Elzeth.

Only he couldn't find the foundation.

He'd envisioned the barrier as many things over the years. At times, he imagined it as a brick wall. Other times, it was a veil. The form of the barrier mattered little, but it was the form he obsessed over. It had never occurred to him to worry about where to put it. There had always been Elzeth, a recognizably separate entity within him, and him.

He searched for that boundary, that familiar dividing line, but found nothing. When he turned his attention to his core, he felt Elzeth not as something stirring within but as a flame consuming him from the inside. The fire burned away the walls of separation.

"Elzeth!" He called for the sagani, but there was no answer from within.

"Elzeth!" He focused harder on the call, though it shouldn't make a difference. Elzeth was always there, always attuned to the world, so he could stir himself to action if needed.

Now Tomas felt only the flame, always spreading, devouring everything it touched.

Tomas tried again to build the walls between him and Elzeth, but whenever he tried to build the first layer, power washed it away. It was like trying to cook a meal when a group of hungry children kept stealing ingredients. Without a foundation, there was nowhere to build.

His senses were too sharp. The wind driven before the incoming storm stabbed into his skin like needles. Every flash of lightning blinded him, and every roll of thunder deafened him. He squeezed his eyes shut and covered his ears, but it hardly made a difference.

He was on the verge of surrendering when he felt the first definite movement from Elzeth. The sagani felt like a small stone in his stomach, tossed and turned by the fiery currents that burned deep in his core. But it was the sagani who found the boundary, who staked the first piece of the barrier into place as though he was a settler claiming a new homestead as his own.

Tomas rushed toward the foundation, throwing brick after brick on top. They wobbled and fell, the barrier burning away almost as fast as they could build. But they both piled on, and with every level they built, the construction became easier. Every inch helped Elzeth to solidify and to separate. With the separation came control, and the fires within his core finally flickered out.

Their success did little to reassure Tomas. His heart still

thudded in his chest, kicking against his ribcage like it was trapped and trying to escape. A soft rain fell, mixing with a few tears as it splashed on his face. He wasn't sure if his tears were relief or fear, but he let them fall. His breathing was fast and shallow, and he forced himself to slow down and fill his lungs.

He needed to talk to Elzeth about what had happened, but he couldn't bring himself to do it. The sagani was silent, and Tomas basked in the feeling of just being himself. The familiarity of self seemed a strange thing to celebrate, but after it had almost been forcefully stripped away, it was as comforting as a roaring fire on a winter's night.

The rain started to fall harder, and Tomas went to wipe the water from his brow. As he did, his right hand suddenly twitched, and he almost smacked himself in the face.

Tomas stopped and stared at his hand, eyes wide. It spasmed again, and he clutched it to his chest, cursing the fates.

20

Q uinton raised his right arm and made a giant circle with his hand. He shook it out, then made a fist and released it several times. The demon had healed him well, and when he next met Tomas, he would be ready.

At least, he hoped he would be.

He hadn't expected whatever Tomas had become. It stunk of madness, but that simple answer didn't satisfy him. Tomas had fought similarly to their last battle outside of Chesterton after he'd contacted the nexus. He'd been even faster and stronger today, though his technique had suffered as a result.

If not for the Family assassin, Ghosthands rather suspected he would be dead at the moment. He looked across the street to where the assassin was licking his wounds. "Thank you for the help."

He couldn't bring himself to bow, but the assassin still deserved his gratitude.

The assassin rotated left and right, testing his own healing. To Quinton's eye, the other man had been good to fight for a bit now. He was younger than Quinton and probably a victim of the demons for less time. It stood to reason that he would burn a little brighter.

"Not doing it for you, old man. I just don't want you or Tomas to win, and the only way I see that happening is by helping you for a bit. I'll still kill you once it doesn't cost me the woman."

"Of course. I don't suppose you have a name, do you? If we're going to be working together."

"I do have a name, but I don't part with it easily. You can call me Xavier."

"Well, thank you, Xavier, for helping me. I'm not sure I would have survived that without you."

"About that. That wasn't the same Tomas I met earlier. Is he going mad?"

"I'm not sure, but I agree. He's gotten much stronger, and I'm not sure why."

Xavier twisted again, grimacing as he did. Quinton couldn't tell if the move was an act designed to lull him into a false sense of confidence or if something about his wounds was bothering him more than Quinton would have expected. Regardless, Xavier didn't seem like he was in a hurry to move.

"When you fought him, it seemed personal," Xavier said. "Why do you hate him so much?"

"He's a host. He's defiled his body, the most precious gift bestowed upon him by the Creator, with a demon. Why shouldn't I hate him?"

The assassin scratched behind his ear and rubbed his neck like Quinton was forcing him to solve a complex puzzle. "But aren't you a host as well? What kind of sense does that make?"

"I know what I've done. I defiled myself intentionally so

that I could be of greater service to the Creator. Tomas and I are nothing alike."

The assassin shook his head. "You're a strange one, Quinton. Do you flinch every time you look in a mirror?"

Quinton didn't dignify that with an answer, and Xavier finally finished his stretching. "So, I think I'm good now. How are we going to do this? I'm assuming you've got at least a handful of knights with you."

Quinton kept his face even. He had not just the knights but the inquisitor-priest in town disguised as a harmless traveler. But he wouldn't reveal anything he didn't need to. "And given that you had a few rifles with you in Razin, I'm guessing you aren't alone here either. Where do you have them?"

The assassin chuckled. "Yeah, I'm not going to tell you that."

Quinton considered their situation. "What if we cooperated? They have at least thirty soldiers with rifles, which is a difficult escort to defeat even with my knights. If your rifles are any good, they might make all the difference."

The assassin squatted and scribbled in the dirt of the road with his finger. He thought out loud. "I don't know exactly where your knights are, but I can guess they're somewhere closer to the train, where their lack of rifles makes less of a difference. My own rifles are closer to the outskirts of town, where the rifles have the most range. I think that's all we need to know."

Quinton had already guessed as much, so the sliver of information meant little. There was obviously more Xavier wasn't saying, but there wasn't much he could do about it.

"So, we expect that the knights and the rifles are enough to hold back the army. That just leaves Tomas. What should we do about him?"

The solution was straightforward enough. "We need to hunt him down. He'll be trying to find the knights and probably your rifles so that the army can enter without a problem. We need to stop him before he succeeds."

"So, east it is?"

"East it is."

Quinton and Xavier slogged their way east. The rain had started to fall, but the worst of the storm was still a way off. Before long, though, the reduced visibility would make Xavier's rifles less effective. The same would be true of the army escort, but they had more to gain as they approached the fortified position.

Even moving slowly, it didn't take them long to discreetly check their positions. They briefly separated with a promise to shout if they spotted Tomas, then checked on their respective allies. The knights reported no sightings. Quinton urged vigilance, then broke off contact. He wandered to the pre-arranged meeting point. He didn't have to wait long. Xavier appeared not long after, equally calm.

"Nothing?" Quinton asked.

"They haven't seen anything."

Quinton shielded his eyes and glanced up at the sky. The clouds loomed darker to the west, constantly lit by the lightning arcing across their bottoms. "The army is going to have to make their move soon. Where is he?"

"Maybe we hurt him worse than we thought." Xavier's faltering answer spoke volumes about his doubts, doubts Quinton shared. Tomas had fought too well. They'd drawn blood but accomplished little else.

Quinton examined his own assumptions. Was there

some other method for Tomas and the army to get Rachel onto the train? Nothing besides trying to sneak her aboard made any sense, and that was as daring a move as he could imagine. Even if Tomas was that foolish, Quinton wasn't particularly worried. The inquisitor waited outside the train, prepared for just such a ploy.

His gut told him something else was happening. Tomas's strength, combined with the way he fought, made Quinton assume the wandering swordsman was finally going mad. Maybe he'd already fallen off that cliff. For as long as he'd been a host, it stood to reason his descent would be a quick affair.

"Why are you smiling?" Xavier asked.

Quinton hadn't even realized he had. But the satisfaction he felt at the thought of Tomas falling into madness and failing his friends was like a potent drug. The Creator was good, indeed, to punish the wicked for their sins. "I think Tomas is going mad."

Xavier's eyes narrowed. "Why is that a source of such joy? The same fate awaits you, if you live long enough."

Quinton shook his head. Joy filled him from crown to toe. There was a lesson here for him to take to heart. He'd thought so long and so hard about how he would kill Tomas before the Creator ended his service. But he needn't have worried. The Creator was always in control, always moving humans around to exactly where they needed to be. And Quinton was exactly where he needed to be right now. He was here with a purpose.

"You're wrong about me," he said.

Xavier took half a step back, wary, and he was right to.

"I will never go mad. Before my time comes, Father will end my service, and I will be allowed to take my own life."

Xavier's hands went to his daggers. "You hate hosts that much?"

"How can you not? Can't you feel the demon crawling in your skin, trying to make you its own?"

Xavier didn't draw his daggers, but he looked ready. "The sagani saved my life. They left me for dead after a feud, and it gave me more years with those I care about. It gave me the strength to serve the Family, as well as my loved ones. I'll never be able to express my gratitude appropriately."

The assassin didn't understand. None of them did. The Creator and His purposes were beyond their worldly concerns. Cooperating with the assassin had been a mistake, a moment of weakness. The Creator had Porum and the train well in hand. But the Creator had turned even Quinton's weakness to His own purposes, and now a demon stood before him, ready for slaughter.

Quinton drew his sword. First, he would dispose of this demon, and then he'd make sure that Tomas was dead or so mad he could no longer help his friends.

He laughed as he cut at the assassin.

21

Tomas found shelter in one of Porum's many abandoned houses. Rain tapped against the roof as distant lightning flickered through the dirty, cracked windows. He sat in a corner of an empty room, legs crossed, the back of his head pressed against the wall. His traitorous hands rested on his knees as he tried to remember the practices that had served him for so long.

He fought a losing battle. Elzeth was a storm inside his stomach, twisting and kicking like an animal in a cage. The sagani's emotions bled together with his own, and Tomas wasn't sure where his feelings ended and the sagani's began.

"Why now?" he asked Elzeth.

The sagani didn't answer. In all their years together, Tomas didn't think he'd ever sensed Elzeth so agitated. The sagani felt less like a friend and more like a wild animal he was trapped with. All the techniques Tomas used to focus failed against the tempest raging in his core.

It didn't help that his heart wasn't in it. His hands were still now, but he hadn't imagined the tics. His time was finally running out, and despite knowing this day had been coming for years, he wasn't ready. Ghosthands was here, eager to kill him and steal Rachel back to the church she was trying to flee. Angela and the others were about to charge into an ambush. They needed him, now more than ever, but he couldn't convince his limbs to move.

"We need to get out there while we still can," Tomas said.

His words fell on deaf ears. The sight of his hands twitching had turned his insides to ice and brought tears to his eyes, but his struggles paled compared to the emotions coursing through Elzeth.

Tomas had never had children nor been particularly interested. But Elzeth felt the way he imagined a two-year-old did when their favorite toy had been taken away. His old friend was throwing a tantrum, destroying everything he could touch. Elzeth burned for a few moments, then turned icy cold. In one breath, Tomas would feel almost as strong as an ox. The next even standing seemed a chore.

"Elzeth!" Tomas shouted.

The sagani continued to ignore him. Tomas briefly considered stabbing himself just to get Elzeth's undivided attention. He discarded the idea, afraid it was a sign of the madness nibbling away at the edges of his sanity. He settled for shouting again.

Finally, the sagani calmed down enough to speak. "What?"

Elzeth sounded as sullen as an infant, too, but Tomas was just glad to be talking to him again. "What's wrong, friend?"

The question set off another tantrum, but this one didn't last long. Elzeth mastered himself, and he felt once again like the friend Tomas had spent so much of his adult life with. Even so, Tomas sensed Elzeth's struggle to face his fears long enough to speak of them.

"I can feel myself fading," Elzeth said.

Tomas sensed there was more and kept quiet.

"Even in unity, I always have some sense of who I am. There's always me and you, and though unity erases the boundary between us, there's still a me in there somewhere. Not that time, though. I was gone. You felt it, too, didn't you?"

Tomas nodded. He suspected the feeling wasn't as strong for him. They were both embodied in his body, a physical sense of identity Tomas could hold on to even during unity. Elzeth lacked that. When that last unity had brought them closer than ever, it had left the sagani with nothing.

"I—I can't do that again," Elzeth said. He sounded afraid, but determined, too. "I won't do that again. It's a minor miracle we could separate at all. If we unify again, I'm as good as dead, and everything that makes you *you* will be gone, too."

Tomas couldn't argue with any of Elzeth's points. They'd been lucky to break apart from unity, and it had pushed Tomas one dangerous step toward madness. He didn't know a gambler alive desperate enough to bet that Tomas and Elzeth could separate successfully again. There was only one problem.

"If we're going to fight Ghosthands, or that Family assassin, we need unity. We're not strong enough otherwise."

Elzeth didn't budge an inch. "You've still got the nexus. That will have to be enough."

"I don't think it will be."

"It will have to be. Tomas, this isn't a debate. If I get any sense at all that you're going to tear down the barriers between us, I'll immediately go as cold as I can."

Tomas snarled. "I could force you. It's still my body."

Now their positions were reversed. Elzeth had found his center and was calm, while Tomas fought against the anger that threatened to consume him. After all their fights and sacrifices for one another, Elzeth's refusal to allow unity felt like the deepest betrayal of them all.

Elzeth didn't rise to the provocation. "Perhaps. But I'll still be fighting you, and if you're in a battle with the church and Family assassins, even a moment of distraction will end it all."

Tomas didn't detect a hint of a bluff in Elzeth's tone. "You're serious, aren't you? That you will do everything in your power to prevent unity, even if it means sacrificing Angela and Rachel?"

"I would rather die as myself than live as something else. It's more important to me than anything. More important than Angela and Rachel."

Tomas closed his eyes and brought his breathing under control. "You're going to be the one that kills us both," he said.

"You're not mad at me because you disagree. You're mad because I'm saying the exact things you're too cowardly to admit you believe," Elzeth answered.

Tomas barely kept a lid on his temper. "I wouldn't put myself over Angela and others like you are."

"Of course you would. You might lie to yourself, but you can't lie to me. You know why you fear madness more than death?"

"No, why don't you enlighten me?" Tomas growled.

"Because you'd rather have it all end and go through the gate as yourself than live on as something else."

Tomas felt like he couldn't breathe, like Elzeth had gained a physical form and was a snake tightening around his neck. He swore at the sagani with every curse he could think of but to no avail. Elzeth remained calm. He'd decided on his path and was going to drag Tomas along no matter the fight he put up.

Finally, Tomas surrendered. Elzeth had him in a bind he didn't see a way out of. "You'll cooperate, so long as we stay short of unity, right? You'll burn as hot as you can so long as we remain separate."

"Of course. I'm not against you, old friend. I'm looking out for what we both want."

Tomas almost argued again but let the comment slide. They had more important worries. He pushed himself to his feet and looked out the window. From the approaching darkness of the clouds, Tomas suspected the worst of the rain was about to arrive. The regular lightning made the darkness almost as bright as day.

It was the sort of day Tomas dreamed about sitting out on an enormous sheltered porch, a bottle of ale in his hand, watching the storm roll in. The rain usually fell straight down, except for when a gust of wind funneled through the houses and pushed it sideways. No small part of him wanted to just sit and relax in the abandoned house and let the storm wash over him.

"We need to find the ambush before Seth, Angela, and the army arrive," Tomas said.

The words were barely out of his mouth when he heard the shot of a rifle in the distance. More shots followed moments after.

In response, there was another volley of shots, quieter than the first.

"Sounds like the battle has already started," Elzeth said.

"You ready?"

"Of course."

Tomas strode to the front door, then froze with his hand on the knob. He squeezed tightly but couldn't twist the knob.

"What's wrong?" Elzeth asked.

"You've noticed the tics. I can barely control my hand when they hit."

There was no appropriate answer. Both of them knew it, but Elzeth was the one that put words to it. "What will be will be. If this kills us, so be it. We'll die with a sword in our hands, just as we imagined we would. Head high, old friend. It's been an honor."

The words and gentle warmth of Elzeth's reassurance melted the ice that locked Tomas in place. He twisted the knob, and the door opened, squealing on rusted hinges. "That it has."

Together, they stepped out into the storm, shutting the door to the house behind them. Rain drenched Tomas immediately, but he turned east and ran toward the battle.

22

Tomas wiped the rain from his eyes as he ran toward the gunfire. Now that he was out in the open, it sounded as though the ambushers were firing from two different locations. Tomas avoided the thoroughfare, anticipating knights lying in wait.

The sound of clashing steel brought him to a sudden stop. He pressed himself against the corner of a building and poked his head around. Ghosthands and the Family assassin were dueling, their swords flinging bloody rain as they cut at each other.

"Guess their alliance didn't last very long," Elzeth remarked.

"You won't hear me complaining," Tomas said. He waited until their duel had taken them out of sight, then ran across the intersection toward the ambushers. Gunshots cracked the air more frequently than the lightning, telling Tomas all he needed to know about the battle. He guessed there were three rifles in each of the two buildings near the eastern edge of Porum. They might have been on the rooftops, but Tomas doubted it. They would have known the storm was coming, and the roof was barely a better angle than an upper-level window.

He approached the building closest to him first, the one farther to the north. Its main entrance was to the east, but a small back door faced west. Tomas searched the windows for danger, then ran to the door. He pushed on the latch, but it wouldn't budge. He pressed some of his weight against the door, but he might as well have been trying to push a boulder out of his way. It felt too sturdy for a mere door. The building had clearly been built to serve as a shop on the bottom level, with rooms to live above it. No one had built it to withstand a battle.

Tomas pressed harder, and Elzeth contributed some of his strength. He pushed near the top and bottom corners of the door. The top bent in a little, but the bottom was sturdy.

"You think they barricaded themselves in?" Elzeth asked.

"Seems that way." If he'd had more time, he would have lit the building on fire, but trying to get it to burn with what he had on hand in a driving rainstorm was as good as impossible. He was tempted to kick at the door, but if he made too much noise, he'd lose the element of surprise. He looked around for other entrances, but nothing caught his attention.

They didn't have time for this.

Elzeth burned brighter at Tomas's command. Tomas took a few steps back, then sprinted at the back of the building. He leaped, crossed his arms over his head, and smashed through one of the back windows. He landed and rolled across the shattered glass, ignoring the cuts as he came to his feet.

An enormous iron stove sat to his right, with counters

running along the lengths of the wall. Tomas imagined a team of cooks preparing meals for hungry guests.

Right now, it was dark and cold, with rain pouring through the shattered window. Footsteps pounded on the floor above. Tomas ran out through the only interior door and found himself in a large room filled with empty tables. Above him, footsteps hurried toward the north side of the building. Tomas's gaze followed the sound, revealing a narrow hallway.

He sprinted into the hallway, slammed around a corner, and found himself in another hallway with a stair descending on his right. He ran forward, intending to grab the banister, whip around, and run up the stairs.

The footsteps beat him. He got to the first stair and looked up in time to see two rifle barrels pointed at him. He flattened himself against the stairs as both of the riflemen pulled their triggers. The bullets whined over his head, and he was on his feet running up the stairs as the shooters chambered their next shots.

Tomas drew his sword and slapped at the rifle of the faster shooter. The bullet missed Tomas by a few inches, but then he was too close to shoot. He drove the point of his sword through the faster shooter's chest, then spun to address the second man as the first fell.

The second shooter had the wherewithal to realize his rifle was pointless, but he wasn't nearly skilled enough or fast enough for it to serve as a club. Tomas's sword snaked within his defense easily.

Tomas extended his senses after the second body fell, relying on Elzeth to sharpen his hearing. Another hallway was at the top of the stairs, with closed doors running down both sides. He could eliminate the west-facing rooms entirely, but that still left four rooms to check on the east.

There.

The sound of a woman breathing hard.

Echoes of gunshots from down the street reminded Tomas that he needed to hurry. He had minutes, at most, before the army reached the streets of Porum. He walked toe-heel-toe down the hallway, testing a fraction of his weight against the wood before putting the rest of it down. The woman's breathing was clear enough. She hid in the third room on the right.

Just before he reached the door, his concentration lapsed for a moment, and he put his full weight down without checking the boards first. The floor groaned under his weight.

A bullet tore through the wall, inches in front of where Tomas stood. He cursed and hoped this door wasn't barricaded like the ones downstairs. He ran as another bullet cut through the space he'd been standing.

The door broke open as Tomas lowered his shoulder and slammed through. The woman within snapped her rifle around, but Tomas was too fast and too close. He cut her down before she could get off another shot, then raced to the window.

He swore again when he saw the army escort clearly through the driving rain. They were charging hard. The rifles in the building farther to the south fired as quickly as the shooters could cycle the bolts. Horses screamed as they fell. Army shooters responded, but shooting from a galloping horse was pointless.

The Family rifles continued their barrage, ignoring the army's violent retort. Tomas watched another two horses and riders fall, then sprang into action. He climbed out the open window, fingers barely finding purchase against the rain-soaked wood. He pulled himself onto the roof and hurried over to the edge of the building. The distance to the other building was maybe fifteen paces.

The jump was near the limit of his distance, but he didn't have the time to assault the building like he had this one. He needed to silence those rifles. Grabbing the nexus would have given him strength, but he didn't trust his control. He took a handful of steps back to get a running start.

Elzeth burned obediently, filling Tomas's legs with the strength he needed. He sprinted across the rooftop, planted his foot on the lip of the roof, and leaped across the void.

For a moment, he feared he'd misjudged the strength needed, but he fell quickly toward one of the upper-story windows. He tucked in his knees and crossed his arms in front of his face. He hit the window a little low, catching his feet on the lower sill. Glass shattered as he broke through. His landing wasn't as smooth as he'd imagined. The hit against the window frame pitched him forward, and though he tried to roll, the result was more of a mildly acrobatic flop.

Elzeth's strength kept him from feeling most of the pain, but he looked down and saw that he was bleeding from a dozen slight cuts.

That was all he had time to notice before the wall erupted in gunfire. Bullets punched through the walls, though none were too close. Tomas chose one hole and ran toward it, lowering his shoulder and hoping he didn't run straight into a stud.

Another volley shot through the wall before Tomas reached it, and one bullet grazed his head. Tomas ignored the line of fire that burned above his ear. He hit the wall and broke through. He lost his footing and rolled across the ground. The rifles fired again, deafening in the small space. Tomas wished he'd stuffed cotton in his ears.

Family bullets weren't the only danger. The army escort, ignorant of Tomas's efforts, continued pouring lead into the building. The room filled with dust and debris.

But Tomas was among the snipers now, and once he drew his sword, the battle drew toward its inevitable conclusion. He killed two out of the three, and the last died from a lucky bullet shot from outside.

Tomas fought the impulse to go to the window and signal the escort. They would only see a shadow moving in the room and focus their rifles on him. Instead, he crawled out of the room as bullets passed overhead. Once he was safe in the hallway, he hurried down the stairs.

As he'd guessed, the doors were both barricaded, and Tomas didn't have the time to pull one apart. He opened a window and crawled out, slowly emerging into the thoroughfare with his hands raised. The army immediately trained several rifles on him, but the soldiers had the discipline not to fire. Once they recognized him, they turned their weapons away.

Tomas was glad he'd hurried. He was barely in time to catch Seth as the commander galloped down the street. Angela rode beside him, and Tomas squashed the twinge of jealousy that rose in his heart. More than anything, he was glad she had survived.

"There's another ambush up ahead," he said. He had to repeat himself over a crack of lightning and an immediate roll of thunder. "Do you want to get out of the rain for a moment?"

Seth wasn't interested. "Describe the ambush."

"I haven't seen it myself, but I assume there are knights up ahead."

Seth considered for a moment. "Then we'll ride through them. We brought your horse, if you want it."

"Thanks, but I prefer my own feet."

"Suit yourself." Seth gave the order to charge, and they rode hard deeper into the town.

Somehow, the rain came down even harder than before. Wind whipped the water around, and Tomas found that no matter what way he turned, the rain was stinging his face. Tomas kept his eyes open for any sign of either the Family assassin or Ghosthands, but they were nowhere to be found. With any luck, they had killed each other, though Tomas very much doubted he was that fortunate.

It didn't take them long to find the knight's ambush. They had piled a tower of assorted junk high in the middle of the street. Seth halted his advance as soon as he saw it. Tomas looked around, wondering how the knights would use the obstruction to their advantage.

He didn't have long to wait. He'd expected that they would use the obstruction as some sort of fortification, but the knights revealed they had other plans. Moments after Seth called the stop, knights attacked the rear of the column.

The timing couldn't have been more perfect. Halting the advance had drawn everyone's attention toward the obstruction, and although Seth's rearguard returned quickly to their duties, it allowed the knights a few precious moments to advance. That was all they needed to cause havoc.

Sometimes Tomas forgot just how skilled the average knight was. Because almost none were hosts, they lacked the strength and speed to win against a trained host, but Tomas would choose a knight over an untrained host in almost any duel. As disciplined as Seth's soldiers were, they couldn't hold a candle to the skill of a single knight.

The rearguard had fallen by the time anyone realized there was a problem. The constant rain, lightning, and thunder forced Tomas to dull his senses, so even he didn't notice the attack until one soldier got a shot off. He turned to see the knights advancing through the column, cutting down soldiers as they ran. They ran past the rear-most wagon without bothering to check within.

The details of the ambush clearly favored the knights. Though they carried only swords compared to the escort's rifles, the column was packed in close as it made its way down the thoroughfare. Many of the soldiers couldn't fire out of fear of hitting their friends. By the time they had a clear shot, the knights were often within sword range. Some of the more clear-thinking escorts flung their rifles over their shoulders to draw swords, but none had the knight's skill with the weapons.

Tomas drew his sword and ran back down the column. Angela dismounted from her horse as she drew her sword, but he had no time to worry about her. Another two soldiers died before he could reach the knights, but he finally met them near the second wagon.

The knights saw him coming but didn't stop cutting their way through Seth's soldiers. Tomas noted it and recognized that something more was behind the knights' actions, but couldn't guess what. He crossed swords with the first knight and was surprised to find himself forced back a step. He worried for a moment that he'd come across another contingent of host-knights, but as he set his feet and focused on the battle, he realized that wasn't the case. The knight was strong, but didn't host a sagani. Tomas wasn't as strong as he should have been.

The second knight walked past the first without coming to his friend's aid. He kept killing soldiers as fast as he could reach them, and Tomas's full attention was on the first knight.

Tomas was in a hurry to attack, and so he thrust harder than he should have. His right foot slipped in the mud. Thankfully, the knight retreated to avoid the cut, and Tomas regained his balance before the next pass. But the knight's eyes had traveled to Tomas's foot. He'd noticed and would no doubt attempt to bait Tomas into another foolish attack.

The knight offered the opportunity a moment later, an opening so tempting it had to be a trap. Tomas resisted the urge, waiting for a better time. Behind him, another soldier fell from their horse with a cry.

At Tomas's command, Elzeth burned brighter. The sagani wasn't pleased about it, but they were well short of unity, so Tomas ignored the sagani's resentment. The difference proved crucial. In the next pass, Tomas deflected the knight's sword enough off its line that he could land a killing blow. The knight wobbled and fell to one knee, and Tomas decided that was good enough. He turned to find the knight's partner and was horrified to see how far he'd gotten.

Tomas bounded after him, and the knight either didn't notice or didn't care, because he never lost his focus on his next victim. Tomas cut the other knight down with one strike, then turned his attention to the other side of the caravan, where the other two knights fought a very different battle.

Angela was remarkable. She was a skilled sword, though not so good as either of the knights. She, along with two fast-thinking soldiers, had formed a wall the knights were having trouble fighting their way past. Angela fought in front of the soldiers while they fired whenever they thought they had an open shot. The knights hadn't died yet, but they weren't making progress.

Tomas came around from the other side of the second wagon and attacked from behind. The first knight he killed never realized he was there, but the second turned as soon as his friend fell.

The second knight attacked Tomas. They crossed swords, and the knight ended up retreating right into Angela. She added her sword to Tomas's, and together they overwhelmed the knight.

It was the first time they'd truly fought together since he'd first come to Razin, and he'd forgotten how powerful of a drug the feeling could be. Too often, he felt like he was forced to take on the role of a protector. Not that he didn't feel protective of Angela, but she was one of the few people he knew who could stand on her own and keep her head in dangerous situations.

That was one of the biggest reasons it had been so hard to leave her behind.

If she allowed it, he didn't think he would ever leave her again.

He pushed the thoughts aside to focus on their more pressing problems. The caravan wouldn't be able to advance through the obstruction the knights had built, and Tomas wasn't sure the wagons would make it through Porum's narrower streets. Once he was sure there were no more knights, he hurried over to Seth.

The commander looked distraught. The composure that had so impressed Tomas earlier had cracked, revealing itself as a façade. He had many of his surviving soldiers huddled around him, and no orders escaped his lips.

Tomas spoke first. "We need to abandon the wagons. We'll go faster on foot from here."

"If we leave the horses behind, we're leaving a lot of options behind," Seth argued.

Tomas took that to mean that if they left the horses behind, the only way was forward, and Seth didn't like not having the option to retreat. He didn't dare call out Seth's cowardice in front of his soldiers, though. Long experience had taught him it would never end well. "That's true, sir, but the train isn't far away. We can run there on foot a lot faster than we can get there with the wagons. I don't know how many more forces there are in Porum, but the faster we get to the train, the fewer chances we give them to strike."

Tomas watched Seth weigh the options. The commander's eyes kept darting to the caravan and to the number of dead soldiers who lay unmoving in the street. Tomas sensed the decision would not go his way. Seth had lost more here than he'd ever lost before, and he was more focused on not losing another soul than he was on finishing the mission.

Tomas respected the sentiment well enough. He'd much prefer to serve under a commander who valued the lives of his soldiers over one who threw them into battle without the slightest concern for their safety. But the stakes here were too high, and failure was unacceptable. Rachel was too important.

He tried again. "Sir, I believe that I have killed most, if

not all, of the Family assassins and the knights. I suspect a few powerful enemies are still in town, but we'll have far better luck defending against them if we can get to the train. The longer we stay out in the open, the more dangerous it is."

Angela chimed in behind Tomas. "For what it's worth, I agree, sir. Our greatest safety is reaching the train quickly."

Tomas wanted to say more but feared that he had already pushed too hard. Seth wavered, then deflated. It was only for a moment, and then the façade returned, but Tomas didn't doubt that almost every one of his soldiers had seen it. Still, when Seth spoke, his voice rang out clear above the storm. "I agree. Soldiers, dismount! We're walking to the train."

24

Quinton raged as he cut at the Family assassin. What he wanted, more than anything, was to cut that damned smirk off the man's face. But like Tomas, the assassin seemed unfamiliar with the idea that he was supposed to die. Quinton had caught him with several cuts that should have at least slowed him, but the assassin healed faster than anyone Quinton had ever fought. He feared that even a stab through the heart wouldn't prove sufficient.

His own wounds didn't heal so quickly. The assassin's daggers had sought his arteries and his lungs, and it had taken nearly every trick Quinton had ever learned to keep him away. The assassin wasn't particularly strong, but his speed was incredible.

Quinton snarled at Xavier, hoping to lure the assassin in, but Xavier danced away, the smirk never leaving his face. "Why won't you fight me?" Quinton yelled.

"I'm waiting for you to return to your senses so we can fight Tomas together."

The answer enraged Quinton further, and he cut at

Xavier's neck. Xavier dodged back with ease, but Quinton pressed, careful to keep his balance in the muddy streets.

Xavier continued the retreat, always willing to give up ground to keep himself away from Quinton's sword.

"How much longer are you going to keep this up?" he asked.

"Until you die!"

Xavier sighed as he skipped back from another attack. Quinton lashed out again, and again Xavier retreated. Quinton stopped. He needed a fresh approach. As he considered his options, Xavier cocked his head to the side and frowned.

"Do you hear that?" he asked.

Quinton braced himself, expecting an attack. "Hear what?"

"Exactly."

Quinton frowned, and then the realization hit him. The rifles, which had formed the sonic background of their fight, had fallen silent. Between his focus on his own battle and the nearly constant rumble of thunder overhead, he hadn't noticed. "Did they finish it?"

Xavier shook his head, and Quinton was finally treated to an expression besides that constant smirk. The assassin's eyes flared and narrowed, and the grip on his daggers tightened.

Quinton's heart pounded harder in his chest. Now, finally, the assassin was ready to take the fight seriously. Now Quinton would have his opportunity to kill the assassin and end this farce of an alliance. He would never ally himself with a demon.

Xavier raised one dagger and pointed it at Quinton's heart. "Your foolishness gave Tomas time to interfere."

"He's gone mad!" Quinton cried. The thought filled him

with a giddy glee. "If he's still alive, he's crying in a corner somewhere, haunted by the ghosts of all the innocents he's killed."

Xavier's eyes narrowed further. "Perhaps he is not the one who has gone mad."

The words meant nothing to Quinton. He had his enemy before him, a host who was a killer. The Creator wanted Xavier dead, and Quinton was his sword. He laughed, and the thunder answered above them.

He charged Xavier. The Creator had designed this moment with exquisite care. His life was nothing more than a play that had been scripted from beginning to end, and he was the protagonist, saving the west from the villainy that threatened it.

Yes. It felt right and true. The play only had an audience of one, the Creator himself, who both wrote the play and enjoyed the performance.

And when Quinton exited the stage, when he passed through the gate for good, he knew there was more waiting for him. No Creator would write such a play and leave the star to such an ignominious end. If he played his role to perfection, if he never deviated from the script, something better awaited him on the other side of the gate. The same eternal reward granted to all true believers.

What a performance he would give!

Their clash was different this time. Xavier stayed in close, trying to use his faster daggers to deflect Quinton's sword and punch bloody holes in his stomach. Quinton used his greater strength to push past Xavier's defenses, then relied on his reach to keep away from those deadly daggers.

Cuts opened on both warriors, but it was Xavier that retreated from the press. Quinton grinned, showing all his teeth. The assassin had to recognize the truth. He was nothing but a bit player, an enemy to scare the audience.

Quinton raised his sword. "Surrender, and I will end you quickly."

Xavier shook his head. "Why do you hate us so much when you are one of us? You know there's nothing inherently evil about the sagani. You live with one every day."

"I have mastered one as a tool, the same as I have my sword."

Xavier shrugged, as if to say that he didn't understand the difference.

"The Creator is perfect, and humanity is his greatest creation. We defile ourselves and spit in the face of our Creator when we allow the demons into our bodies. We are meant to serve as more than hosts to demons. That's what madness is, after all—our bodies rejecting the defilement. The evidence stares you in the face, yet you are too great a coward to acknowledge it. What greater service can a believer offer than to kill those who would most defile this creation?"

Xavier took a step back as he realized the truth. He was a fallen creature, and Quinton was his salvation. Quinton expected that with his next movement, he would bow his head and accept his end.

Instead, the assassin turned and ran.

Quinton raged and charged after the assassin, but he lacked the smaller man's speed. The assassin ran for a building, then leaped through a shattered window. Quinton slowed and poked his head through the window before following.

Broken glass lay scattered on the inside, but the blood appeared dry. There was no sign of Xavier. Quinton took a few steps back, got a running start, and leaped through the window, too. His landing crunched the glass underfoot, announcing his arrival to anyone still in the building. He looked around. This was a kitchen, or at least, had been once.

He advanced slowly, senses sharp. Someone moved softly upstairs. Quinton suspected it was Xavier, but there was no guarantee they were alone. The door in the kitchen opened up into a small dining hall, and Quinton guessed he was in an inn. The only sounds of life he heard came from upstairs.

He saw a small hallway off to the side and walked down it, sword ahead of him. Strobes of lightning illuminated the hallway in brief flashes, and it sounded like the storm outside had grown more intense.

He found the first bodies when he turned the corner. Quinton didn't recognize them, but he saw the tattoos that marked them as Family. Between the rifles on the stairs, the bullet holes in the wall, and the wounds on the Family, Quinton easily guessed what had happened.

Had Tomas left anyone alive, or were he and Xavier the only two left?

He strongly suspected the latter. He climbed the stairs, sword ahead. The small rooms and tight hallways favored Xavier's daggers, but Quinton didn't plan on letting the assassin get close.

Quinton heard the sharp intake of breath a moment before one door on the right flung open. It gave him enough time to back away as Xavier charged out of the room. The assassin bounded off the wall on Quinton's right.

There was no hesitation in Xavier's attack nor any mercy. His daggers meant to kill, and Quinton exulted in the duel. The hallway limited their movement, forcing them in close.

Twice Quinton believed he'd made the winning move, only to find Xavier's second dagger deflecting his steel safely away. Sword and daggers met, broke apart, and met again as lightning flashed brightly in the hallway. With no space to retreat and almost no room to maneuver, they could do nothing but rely on their strength and skill.

Quinton's techniques were honed as sharp as his sword. He placed every cut, parry, and stab with a precision a watchmaker would have admired.

Xavier's techniques reminded Quinton more of a roiling river than pure swordsmanship. He crashed against Quinton with all the force of a waterfall, but he never directly resisted. He flowed around Quinton's sword like water rushing around a boulder in the heart of the current. The assassin never remained still long enough for Quinton's superior techniques to triumph. And like a raging river, he wore down the edges of Quinton's defenses, relentlessly poking and prodding, just like a river seeking the one weakness it could exploit to overrun its banks.

Skilled as they were, the fight couldn't last for long.

Xavier's style proved too much for Quinton, and the hallway was too small for Quinton to fight at his best. The assassin finally slipped past Quinton's defense and stabbed a dagger deep into Quinton's thigh.

Quinton roared and sliced down, but Xavier pulled his dagger out and danced backward, well out of reach. Quinton took a step, ready to resume their fight, but his leg wobbled. He could stand, but he couldn't fight.

Xavier studied him for a long moment, then cleaned his daggers and sheathed them.

"Aren't you going to finish me?" Quinton asked, putting as much condescension into his voice as he could. He couldn't reach the assassin, but if Xavier attacked, Quinton could drag one more corrupted soul through the gates with him, and the Creator would smile upon his final offering.

Xavier didn't rise to the bait, though. "I was never here to kill you. The scholar is all I need."

Xavier turned to go.

"Coward!" Quinton shouted.

Xavier waved as he walked away. Quinton took two steps after him, and then his leg finally gave way. Xavier didn't even turn his head.

The assassin went into one room, and Quinton's sharpened hearing heard him step up onto a windowsill and drop into the street below. Then even the sound of him was lost in the storm.

Quinton didn't know how long he lay in the hallway. The demon within him, desperate to maintain the body that served as its home, healed the wound in his thigh, though the healing felt slower than usual. He might have only closed his eyes for a few minutes, but it might have been more like a half-hour.

When his wound was closed and mostly healed, he willed the demon in his flesh to silence. It fought and argued, but it had learned well enough that there was only one master in this relationship. It went still, and Quinton immediately felt sick. He rolled over onto his side and vomited.

Gross as the vomit was, it felt as though he was purging his body of the evils of the demons. When he spit out the last of the acidic taste in his mouth, he felt better.

He wished he could vomit out his memories as easily. The thoughts running through his head during the battle loomed large in his awareness, and he closed his eyes against the truth shining in his face.

It was too soon.

Not because he hadn't been a host for long enough. He hadn't been one for nearly as long as Tomas, but he was well within the end of his expected lifespan.

No, it was too soon because his work wasn't finished yet. Father hadn't given him permission to succumb to madness.

Quinton sat up, groaning as his partially healed leg complained about the movement. He took several deep breaths, feeling the air moving through his lungs.

He wasn't going mad. No, this was just the Creator warning him. The Creator told him he had little time to put his affairs in order. Viewed through that lens, Quinton took comfort. Few people were fortunate enough to know for certain that their death approached. Most were completely ignorant, and they wasted their days and their weeks thinking they had an endless horizon ahead of them. Quinton knew better and with that knowledge, would make the most of his remaining days.

He stood and ground his teeth together as his leg screamed at the abuse. The demon wanted to be let free, to finish healing the leg, but Quinton forcefully restrained it, much as he had when they'd first been joined. Eventually, the demon's fight subsided.

The more Quinton used the demon, the faster his end would come. That didn't mean he would avoid its use. His own life and sanity were nothing but offerings for the Creator. He'd use the demon only when necessary, when its use would provide the Creator with his greatest service.

He leaned against the wall and slowly made his way down the hallway. Every stair sent a flare of pain up his leg, through his spine, and straight to the back of his neck. He gritted his teeth even as the sharp pain brought tears to the corners of his eyes.

Quinton hobbled out into the storm. The streets were quiet, and the worst of the thunder and lightning seemed to be farther to the east. He shuffled down the street, alert for dangers.

He spotted a few curious faces staring at him out of windows, but when he turned in their direction, they disappeared again. He imagined Porum would have quite the mess to clean up, but he didn't care. The future of the church was close to the train or upon it. He wouldn't miss its departure.

A few minutes of painful stumbling later, he found the barricade the knights had set up. From the position of the bodies, it looked like the ambush had worked exactly the way they had planned. The knights, as expected, had acquitted themselves well, but all four were dead in the street. Guilt assailed him at the sight.

If not for the madness, he would have been here, the other half of the pincer that was supposed to close on the escort. Weakened by the rifles of the Family and ambushed from behind by the knights, it had been Quinton's role to stride from the barricade and kill the leaders of the escort.

He wondered if the knights had kept pushing forward. If they'd kept expecting him to come around that barricade and close the trap. Or had they realized, before the end, that he had betrayed them?

The scene presented no answers, and Quinton found the mere thought of the battle troubling, so he pressed on. If the knights were dead, it meant the scholar and at least a few of her escorts had reached the train.

The inquisitor would be on board, so the mission was far from lost. But Quinton needed to be on that train.

He was a block past the barricade when the train whistle blew, long and loud.

Quinton swore. He was still several blocks away from the station. Even if he used the demon, he couldn't heal his leg in time to run and catch the train, and this close to departure, the escort would notice his arrival. There was no chance to blend in with whatever small crowd had gathered.

He thought quickly. The train tracks passed close by, but he didn't think he could run fast enough to catch the train, and the conductor would be wary of stowaways attempting exactly what Quinton imagined.

He imagined the surrounding area, grateful he'd taken the time to study the town well before Tomas and the escort had arrived.

There was one tall building near the line. The jump was too much for a civilian, but with a demon, Quinton could make it.

He considered other possibilities, but nothing more came to mind. Lacking choices, he let the demon loose to continue healing his wound. He walked as the demon worked, finding the building with little difficulty. It was a two-story warehouse next to the train yards. Quinton didn't even have to go inside. A set of stairs led to a door on the second story, and from there, Quinton pulled himself to the roof. He glanced west and saw that the train had already built up its steam.

Another long whistle warned the onlookers to back up, and the train slowly inched forward. Quinton realized he wasn't sure that Tomas and the others were on the train, but he had to assume they were. He'd find out soon enough if not.

He tested his leg, and although it wasn't up to full health, he thought it would support enough of his weight.

With his permission, the demon's strength flowed through his muscles. A considerable amount rushed to the wound, and Quinton examined his own thoughts. They didn't seem unusual, for which he was grateful. The descent into madness wasn't a linear path but a rocky downslope. It didn't give him a false sense of immortality.

When the train reached him, he was ready. He let the engine and the coal car pass him, as well as the first and second passenger compartments. If he'd been in charge of escorting a high-value prisoner, he'd be stationed near the front of the train to prevent enemies from reaching the engine.

When the fourth passenger car neared, Quinton ran and leaped.

For a few moments, it felt as though he were a bird taking wing in the sky. But then he fell. He imagined his legs filled with the demon's strength, but he still hit hard.

Quinton let his legs collapse as another sharp flare of pain ran up his leg. He tumbled and slid, only coming to a stop when he struck a vent. He groaned and swore, but he still had the presence of mind to demand the demon be still.

Perhaps it wasn't the usual way to catch a train, but he was on board.

25

S eth quickly regained the respect Tomas had lost in
him. The commander's losses had sent him into shock,
but he'd emerged with a singular focus on completing his
task.

They had wandered through side streets until they
reached the station, and Seth led them through the station
like a commander leading the charge through enemy lines.
The conductor and engineer were expecting the soldiers,
even if the state of their arrival caused no small amount of
concern. Railroad guards had circled the station with their
rifles, alerted by the vast amounts of gunfire to the east.

There had been a few tense moments, but Seth had
navigated the situation well, and it wasn't long before the
soldiers were taking up station in the first two cars. The
army had either purchased—or forced the railroad to give—
both cars for the army's exclusive use. Had they arrived with
their full contingent, the cars would have been perfect, but
Seth took one look at the cars and ordered everyone to the
first car.

Tomas liked the decision, especially when Seth set up barricades in the second car and stationed soldiers there. Rachel was as safe as any traveler could be.

Tomas watched the rest of the cars as passengers trickled in. Being as this was the end of the line, the train would depart without many passengers, then fill up as it traveled east. Nothing he saw gave him any alarm. A couple of families boarded, as well as a handful of well-dressed men and women who appeared to be merchants.

He kept watch until the train blew its final whistle. He stepped backward onto the train, making sure no one boarded the train at the last moment. Once he was sure they were safe, he retreated into the second passenger car. The soldiers there gave him respectful nods as he worked his way to the first car.

Even though he'd only been on the train for minutes, the journey reminded him of why he disliked them so much. They rocked and rolled like an unruly horse. They smelled of oil and grease and were loud. Though his own two feet were much, much slower, he vastly preferred them as a mode of travel.

Now that they were on the train, he allowed his thoughts to travel to the future. There was no telling how much time was left to him, but it was less than he wanted.

"Something on your mind?"

Tomas startled. He'd crossed from one train car to the next but hadn't even noticed Angela until she spoke.

He almost lied and said, "No," but caught himself. "Thinking a bit about what comes next."

"Aren't you getting ahead of yourself? We still need to get her safely east."

"Sure, but we're on the train, moving faster than any

messages. The church and the Family made their move here, and we fought through them. There shouldn't be too much trouble from here on out."

"Never figured you for such an optimist." Angela sat down on one bench and patted the space next to her. "Want to talk about it?"

He didn't really, but it made more sense to let her know everything so that when he left, she could find some closure. He sat down next to her.

"When I went into Porum to scout, I found both Ghosthands and the Family assassin from Razin waiting for me."

"The same Ghosthands from Chesterton?"

"The one and only." Tomas detailed the fight, then talked about the difficulty in separating from Elzeth. "Once we succeeded, I noticed that I'd developed a tic. It doesn't strike often, but when it does, I can't control my hand."

Angela nodded solemnly. "So, what exactly does that mean?"

"Nothing precise, unfortunately. It just means the madness is closer than ever. Added on top of that, Elzeth is adamant that we never unify again. To be honest, I agree with him."

"So your days as a wandering swordsman are about at an end," Angela concluded.

"Seems that way."

Angela considered for a few seconds, then asked, "So, what were you thinking?"

"Hmm?"

"About what came next?"

"At first I thought that I'd really like to spend what days I have remaining with you. But that doesn't seem right. Even if we could recapture what we shared last time, it's not fair to you. You shouldn't have to watch me fade. Better, I think, to wander alone for a while. When there's little sanity left, I think I'll grab hold of the nexus and let Elzeth escape. He can live on, and I'll die on a day of my own choosing."

He'd expected some affirmation, but Angela went quiet for a long time. Soldiers moved about the car, and Tomas could see Rachel near the very front. But right now, his entire world was focused here, on this bench.

"It seems a shame to die alone," Angela said.

"I won't be. I'll have Elzeth, right until the very end."

She grimaced at that. "Well, whatever happens, maybe don't decide without telling me first. I won't promise anything, but I'm going to think about it."

Angela stood, and he twisted to let her pass. She stepped out into the aisle of the car and stretched.

Tomas stood, too. Angela's words had given him hope, but he wanted to make sure where they stood. "One last thing. If it's pity motivating you, I'd rather you just let me go. I only want to join you if that's what you genuinely want."

"Of course," she said. She brushed some of her hair back behind her ear and walked away. She joined Seth, and they immediately launched into a discussion about something related to their travels.

Tomas stood by the bench for a while, the rocking of the train sending him swaying from side to side. Outside, the storm that had just passed through Porum raged, but within the comfort of the train car, it barely mattered.

Such would be the way of the future. Tomas could see it with ease. People would take trains from place to place instead of walking. They'd build and live in cities. Gradually, they'd move away from the wild Tomas loved so much.

Perhaps it was a good time to go. He was a relic of an earlier age.

He saw Rachel was still alone, so he worked his way down the length of the car to join her. "Mind if I sit?" he asked.

"Not at all."

Tomas sat down next to her. "How are you holding up after everything?"

"It's still hard to believe this is all real. Less than a month ago, I was working away in my lab. I'd only heard rifles a few times before in my life, and never so close."

"All that being true, you seem to be holding up well. And I think we're almost to the point where you shouldn't need to worry anymore."

Her gaze lit up at that. "You think so?"

"I do. The church and the Family seemed to focus their resources on catching you out west, and we're the fastest thing moving now. Assuming we don't have any trouble at our next couple of stops, I'd imagine you'll be able to put most of this behind you."

"Thank you. I'm so grateful for everything." She looked down, and it seemed to Tomas like she was about to cry.

He sympathized. She'd probably seen more death in the last few hours than she'd seen in her whole life. More violence, too. Even survivors carried scars, both visible and hidden, for the rest of their lives.

"Well, if there's anything I can do for you, just let me know. I'm happy to help in whatever ways I can."

"Thank you, I will."

Tomas lingered for a few moments, wishing there was something more he could offer. But he'd already fought to get Rachel here, and perhaps that was enough for now. It didn't feel like it, but he didn't know what else he could do.

He stood, gave her a quick bow, then found an empty bench near the center of the car.

A few minutes later, they broke through the storm. The rain stopped thundering on the roof of the car. They left the lightning behind as the clouds thinned above. It was still a gray day, but it was brighter than before.

Tomas couldn't sit still for long. The train had reached its full speed, chugging along the tracks faster than any horse could gallop. The passenger car rattled and rolled. Tomas paced back and forth, but there wasn't far for him to go.

"You're unsettled," Elzeth observed.

"Not sure why. There are plenty of reasons to choose from, but none of them feel quite right."

"It was too easy," Elzeth said.

That brought Tomas to a stop. Of all the reasons he'd considered, that one hadn't been near the top of his list. Now that Elzeth had pointed it out, though, Tomas knew the sagani had the right of it.

"The ambushes didn't feel complete. Maybe something went wrong, but what is the point of an ambush when you don't send out your strongest warriors?" He thought back to when he'd seen the Family assassin and Ghosthands fighting. But why had they been dueling while their sides launched their ambushes?

"If it's a clever strategy, it's beyond me," Elzeth admitted, "but it seems that something went wrong."

"I agree, but neither the Family assassin nor Ghosthands strikes me as the sort to give up so easily. Unless they killed each other, they would have done anything to get on this train."

"You want to walk it up and down to search for them?"

Tomas considered. "Not really. If they're here, it makes

the most sense to stay close. They want Rachel, and Rachel is here."

He thought about it some more and nodded. Angela was here, and Rachel was too. This was where he was needed.

He feared the train ride would not be as quiet as he had hoped.

26

Quinton crawled carefully down the length of the fourth train car's roof. Rain poured down, but the constant thrumming of the storm against the roof masked whatever sounds he now made. The demon healed his legs as he crawled, and by the time he reached the end of the car, he was ready to fight.

He peered down into the space between the two cars and saw it was empty. Though the platforms on each end of the passenger cars were sheltered by the roof, no one wanted to stand outside in this rain. He twisted around and clambered down the ladder. Ducking under the meager shelter of the roof allowed him to wring some of the water from his clothes and get his bearings. He stood on one leg at a time and jumped back and forth, testing his healing. Both legs held his weight without so much as a twinge. Satisfied, Quinton silenced the demon still burning within. It protested, but he pressed until it capitulated.

He entered the passenger car, realizing he would cause quite a stir. His clothes were soaked, cut, and bloody. But he didn't care what the passengers thought of him. They wouldn't bother a man carrying a sword, and if any fool interfered, they'd regret the decision soon enough.

Quinton found the inquisitor in the fifth car, reading the Creator's Word. Their eyes met, and Quinton gave the man a hint of a nod. The inquisitor returned the gesture, then went back to the Word. Quinton exited out the rear of the car and waited on the platform. The storm was finally abating as the train outran the front. Quinton watched the miles pass beneath him as he stood still and marveled at the ingenuity of humanity. The Creator had made humanity in his likeness and given them the world to spread upon.

And look how humanity had fulfilled the promise of their creation! Today it was trains, but who knew what wonders awaited the next generation? Demons had inhabited this planet long before humans, but they'd never accomplished half as much. Once Rachel was in his grasp, the church would lead humanity to a new shining age of progress.

The door to the car opened, and the inquisitor stepped onto the platform.

"What happened?" the inquisitor asked.

Quinton set aside his wonder at humanity's achievements and focused on more mundane matters. "I met with the assassin from the Family. For a time, we allied against Tomas, but the assassin betrayed us. I was fighting him when I was supposed to be at the ambush. Because of that, Tomas defeated the knights and escorted the army to the train."

The inquisitor absorbed the explanation without comment. Quinton wondered if the man had detected his lie.

Inquisitors were a remarkable species. They mastered the art of blending in to their environment. They could waltz at any ball, talk economics with bankers, and win the hearts of women with a look. An inquisitor always seemed to belong wherever they were found.

Quinton had always lacked something crucial when he attempted the same. Whenever he spoke with strangers, he saw the unease in their eyes and in their mannerisms. At first, he hadn't understood, but he now believed it was because they sensed the killer within him, the part of him always ready for violence. No matter how he tried to hide his nature, he always set off some small primal alarm.

The inquisitors were barely less dangerous than he was, but they cloaked themselves in a mask of civility no one saw through. Even though Quinton knew better, he couldn't help but think of the man standing across from him as harmless.

It was an illusion that inquisitors could shatter with a flick of their wrists. The man's blades were well-hidden, but Quinton knew where they were.

Too late, he realized the inquisitor was staring at him. "Why did you fail?" he asked.

The implication was there, unspoken beneath the surface of his question. That Quinton wasn't up to the task Father had set for him.

"The assassin is as strong as anyone I've ever crossed. He got the better of me."

The inquisitor's gaze never wavered. "You know what I am, so you know what I do. What would you say if I told you I see the signs in your eyes, the signs I've seen so many times before?"

Quinton didn't turn away. "I'd tell you we have a mission to complete."

He didn't reach for his sword, but he was ready. Even if the entire world turned against him, he would see Father's will done. The demon within him simmered, eager to be unleashed once again.

The inquisitor was the first to break eye contact. "Just remember, you may have the favor of Father, but I know what you are, and I'll put you in your place if I need to."

"As the Creator wills."

Quinton returned to looking out over the prairie.

"What do you want to do?" the inquisitor asked.

Quinton thought for a moment. "Has the conductor been through yet?"

"No."

"Are you sure? This train has been traveling for a while now."

The inquisitor fixed him with a hard stare.

"Of course. I'm sorry."

Quinton turned the problem over in his mind. There were a few explanations, but only one seemed likely. "The assassin is most likely aboard, then. Have you seen a smaller man with pale hair?"

The inquisitor shook his head.

"Then he's probably in the last car. He's the first threat we must deal with. You go through first, and when you find him, find someplace behind him to settle. I'll follow a few minutes after. All his attention will be on me. As soon as you have an opening, kill him. Make it count, because you'll only get one chance."

The inquisitor looked as though Quinton had made him swallow something bitter, but he nodded and jumped across to the last car. He went in, and Quinton waited.

That the inquisitor had seen through his madness so easily wasn't necessarily unexpected. After all, inquisitors were the arm of the church that hunted down hosts and questioned them after capture. If anyone would notice the signs, it was an inquisitor. But it was problematic. The inquisitor would file a report, and that report would inevitably reach Father's hands.

The thought gave rise to mixed feelings. Quinton would never dare lie to Father. The next time they met, he would be the first to confess his madness. But he wanted Father to hear it from him first, and only after his work was completed.

It occurred to him that the problem would be neatly solved if the inquisitor died, but he shook that off as a thought coming from the devil inside him. Unless the inquisitor's death served the Creator's purpose, Quinton wouldn't touch him.

Enough time had passed, so Quinton jumped across the gap between the cars and prepared for the battle to come. Once he was centered and focused, he opened the door to the last car and stepped inside.

As in the car before, his attire raised no small number of eyebrows, but the other passengers had the good sense not to say anything. The car wasn't very full, and Quinton saw the inquisitor sitting at the very back.

But he didn't see the assassin. He checked twice, then looked again, just to be sure. He walked down the aisle, checking to see if the assassin was trying to hide under a bench. When he reached the end of the car, he opened the rear door and stepped out.

The assassin wasn't at the end of the train, either.

Quinton had been so sure. He stood on the platform and watched the horizon recede. They hadn't crossed paths with the conductor yet, either.

The door opened again, and the inquisitor exited. "You sure he's here?"

Quinton looked down at the steel platform they stood

on. Then he squatted to get a closer look. There was blood on the wood flooring, closer to the door, where the rain hadn't washed it away.

He stood up.

"He's definitely here. We need to get to the scholar before he does."

27

"Did you hear that?" Elzeth asked.

Tomas opened his eyes. He'd closed them for a bit, not to sleep but to find his center. If he let his mind wander, he'd think of nothing but possible futures with Angela and the knowledge Rachel might unlock. He couldn't afford the distraction. If his intuition was right, they weren't alone on this train, and he was in no condition to fight. He rolled the shard of nexus, wrapped in its handkerchief, between thumb and forefinger. Its song was like a whisper.

"No," he said.

"Something outside, near the rear of the car," Elzeth reported.

Tomas turned around in his seat and looked back. Windows ran up and down the length of the passenger cars, but the front and back of the cars provided less visibility. The only windows there were the small windows in the doors that led to the platforms.

Two sentries stood at the rear door, but the small window only provided them with a limited view. Neither of them seemed alarmed, but Tomas didn't dismiss Elzeth's worries. He stood and took two steps toward the rear door.

A brief shadow appeared to Tomas's left, and then the rearmost window on that side of the train shattered. A dark figure dropped through the window and landed easily in the aisle between the benches.

Tomas had his sword in hand in a moment, but the two guards at the door were dead before they understood the danger they were in. By the time their bodies hit the floor, the dark figure was sprinting down the length of the car, leaving more corpses behind.

Tomas caught a flash of light hair underneath a conductor's cap. He reached into his pocket and grabbed the nexus, holding it tight between his hand and the hilt of his sword.

Tomas had been sitting closer to the front of the car, closer to Rachel. He wanted to advance, but the whole car was in motion. The survivors of the knights' ambush leaped to defend Rachel, led by Seth.

Against the Family assassin, they were little better than practice dummies. Their rifles were poor weapons in the confines of the car, and those smart enough to draw steel only made themselves the assassin's first targets. They were all excellent soldiers, and on the open range, Tomas would have rather had them at his back than almost anyone else. Here, they only delayed the assassin for a few moments.

Tomas couldn't get around the press, and was forced to watch as the assassin cut through the soldiers like a scythe through wheat.

Angela.

She had been near the rear of the car, and Tomas feared the worst. He leaned to the right and saw her, rifle at the ready. She'd escaped the initial assault but couldn't fire for the allies she was more likely to hit. The assassin was among them, his daggers constantly taking life.

When the press lessened, Tomas opened himself to the nexus. He lost touch with Elzeth for a moment as the power of the stone ripped them apart, but he trusted the sagani would find his way back.

Unless, Tomas realized with a start, Elzeth decided it was time to return to the nexus. The sagani knew how close to the end they were, how it was riskier than ever to stay with Tomas.

When he felt Elzeth's presence clearly again, Tomas let out a sigh of relief.

"Worried I was going to leave?" Elzeth asked.

"A bit, yeah."

"Don't. I'll tell you when I'm going."

The power of the nexus filled Tomas, though not the way it did when he and Elzeth were unified. Tomas shoved aside two of the remaining soldiers standing in his way.

The assassin grinned at Tomas's arrival. "Miss me?"

Tomas answered with his sword. He advanced, his footing poor. The car floor was soaked with blood and filled with bodies and the still-shifting forms of soldiers who hadn't yet found their way through the gate. Added to all of that, the car continued to rock, the motion never quite the same.

Fortunately, the assassin's position was no better. When Tomas's first assault pressed him back, he stumbled over a corpse he'd created not moments before.

The two soldiers Tomas had saved saw the stumble as their opportunity to leap in and help. Tomas shouted at them as they pushed him aside. They ignored the warning, their thoughts only for the vengeance they wanted to visit on the man who had killed so many of their friends.

Not only did they push Tomas back, but they surrounded the assassin too closely for Angela to fire. The battle was as short as it was certain. The assassin killed them, then ducked for cover as Angela fired.

Angela stepped out into the aisle, intending to get closer, but Tomas held up a hand to stop her. He glanced back. Only four soldiers remained in this car, and they formed a tight circle around Rachel.

"Stay!" he ordered.

They all nodded eagerly, and he suspected he probably hadn't needed to tell them. They'd just watched most of their company die at the hands of one man.

Tomas couldn't see the assassin anymore. He stepped back until his footing was better. "You might as well surrender. You're not getting out of this."

There was no reply to his suggestion, but he hadn't expected there to be one.

Gunshots rang out, but not from this car. The soldiers at the barricade in the next car were shooting at someone, and from the sound of it, they weren't hitting their target.

Was Ghosthands here, too?

Tomas swore. He'd hoped at least one of the other hosts would have had the decency to die.

His moment of distraction almost proved fatal. The Family assassin appeared like a ghost from between the benches and launched himself at Tomas.

Thanks to the speed granted to him by the nexus, Tomas deflected the first dagger, but the second cut him next to his armpit as the assassin crashed into him. They went down hard onto a bench, the assassin on top.

The assassin tried to stab Tomas, but Tomas lifted his hips and threw the assassin forward. He hit face-first, hard, against the window, and Tomas tried to slide out between his legs.

The assassin squeezed his legs together and twisted, sending them both onto the floor of the car.

Tomas was no stranger to grappling, but he was trapped in the small space between two benches. The assassin raised a dagger, and there was nothing Tomas could do to stop it.

A rifle shot echoed louder than any thunderclap in the confines of the car, and the assassin jerked to the side.

Tomas reached out with his right hand and grasped the leg of one bench. He pulled hard, finally sliding out from between the assassin's legs. He was on his feet a moment later, as was the assassin.

Their steel met again, but this time Tomas possessed the upper hand. Angela's bullet had torn through the assassin's left shoulder, leaving it almost useless. Tomas saw fragments of bone as the sagani within pushed them out and tried to heal the wound.

Such wounds didn't close quickly, though, not even for someone who healed as fast as the assassin. Until they did, the assassin was one arm down.

If the assassin had lost, someone had forgotten to tell him, though. He lunged forward, his single dagger moving almost too fast for Tomas to track. Tomas deflected the blade, barely keeping his torso safe. He stepped into the aisle and pushed the assassin back.

The assassin didn't shuffle into the gap between the benches but retreated on top of a bench. He twisted, flinging his useless left arm at Tomas's head. Instinctively, Tomas cut, and the arm flew away, but the assassin had sacrificed the arm for one last blow.

Tomas twisted but knew he wouldn't be in time. He cursed his foolishness.

Another shot rang out, and this time, the impact flung the assassin across one bench and onto the next.

Tomas hadn't seen the point of impact, but he saw the spray of blood as the bullet exited under the assassin's left armpit. He guessed the bullet had gone through the assassin's torso, scrambling his insides until nothing recognizable remained.

Tomas side-stepped down the aisle until he was facing the assassin. The man swore as he repositioned himself so he was propped up by both the bench and the wall of the car. A fresh pool of blood quickly formed under the bench.

"I hate those damn rifles," he said.

Tomas nodded. "I do, too."

The assassin groaned and tried to find a comfortable position. Even in his last moments, he kept a smile on his face. "Figured you would understand. We're not meant for the coming world, are we?"

"I don't think so, no," Tomas said. It was eerie how their thoughts aligned.

The assassin spit out a glob of blood. "Killed by a rifle on a train. Not the way I wanted to go out."

"We rarely get to plan our deaths."

"True enough." The assassin leaned his head back against the window and closed his eyes. "It was fun while it lasted, though."

Tomas could see the host's wounds healing quickly. Normally, he would have assumed Angela's shots were fatal, but the Family assassin had unusual healing abilities.

He raised his sword. "Any last words?"

The man nodded but didn't speak. After a moment, he pushed himself off the bench and slid onto his knees in the middle of the aisle. He looked up at Tomas. "You can't beat him, not as you are."

"Ghosthands?"

The assassin nodded. "He's willing to die for his beliefs, and you're barely willing to live for yours. It's not enough."

"I'll take it under advisement."

The assassin chuckled. "Sure you will."

He bowed his head, exposing his neck for Tomas. "Will you say the words with me?"

"Of course."

They spoke in unison, and their voices filled the car.

"*From the One, we became many*;

To the One we return.

May the gates beyond

Welcome your weary soul."

As soon as the last word was spoken, Tomas brought down the sword. His cut was clean, and the assassin died with a smile on his face.

28

Tomas wanted a few minutes to rest, but he suspected he didn't have the time. As soon as he was sure the assassin was dead, he looked up. "Get away from that door," he ordered Angela.

The shots in the other car had stopped, but Tomas remembered how many the soldiers had fired. Bullets were too expensive to waste, so they were trained not to waste ammunition. Which meant they had been missing.

To Angela's confused expression, he said, "Ghosthands is here, too."

The name got Angela moving. She stopped when she reached the mass of bodies near the center of the car. She crouched down.

"What are you doing?" Tomas asked.

"Looking to see if anyone survived," she answered curtly.

Tomas was ashamed he hadn't even spared a thought for the fallen soldiers. But he was far more worried about what was about to come through that door. He nodded, though Angela wasn't paying any attention to him. He clambered up onto the benches and climbed around her, standing between her and the door.

Nothing came through the door. The silence from the other car was ominous.

If he was assaulting the car, what would he do?

He wasn't sure, but he didn't think he'd come through the front door. It was too predictable. He looked up at the roof.

Tomas turned to the remaining soldiers and pointed to the door connecting the front of the car to the engine. "Lock that door and block it up with whatever you can. Then stay close and keep those rifles pointed toward the rear of the train. Shoot anyone who isn't me."

The soldiers nodded, but no one made any move.

"Now!" Tomas shouted.

That got them moving.

Angela finished her examination of the bodies. Given that she didn't seem to be in any hurry to provide aid, Tomas could guess well enough what she'd learned.

"What are you going to do?" she asked.

"I'm going to find Ghosthands and put an end to this."

She swallowed, then gestured at the Family assassin's body. "I heard what he said before you killed him. Is he right?"

Tomas didn't want to consider the question. "Doesn't matter. I won't let Ghosthands get anywhere near you or Rachel."

Angela looked torn between several responses. Then she shook her head and started reloading her rifle. "Don't you dare die. I'll be right here waiting. I'll take care of Rachel."

"Thanks."

There was so much more that he wanted to say, but he figured that if he wanted to say it, he'd have to survive and return. He went to the back door of the car and opened it. No one waited on the platform.

He stepped onto the platform and took one last look at Angela, who was directing the soldiers. Then he closed the door behind him.

The door on the other car was bouncing open, and Tomas saw the bloodbath that had taken place there. The barricades looked like they hadn't done much good. Tomas watched for a moment but didn't see any movement within. He sheathed his sword, then climbed the ladder.

Ghosthands sat on top of the roof, right near the center of the car. He was cross-legged, and the wind whipped his hair around his face. He seemed at peace as he took in the view. Behind Tomas, the edges of the storm were still visible as a dark smudge against the horizon that flickered with powerful lightning.

Tomas climbed onto the roof. It wasn't the worst footing he'd ever fought on, but it was far from the best. The rocking of the car was more pronounced up here, and the roof always sloped away toward the edge. There was a small lip before falling over, but it wouldn't provide much safety. It explained how the assassin had broken in, though.

"It's glorious, isn't it, Tomas?" Ghosthands asked.

"I'll admit it's a good view."

A smile spread across Ghosthands's lips. There was something different about him. Tomas couldn't place it exactly, but he sensed it.

"It sounds like his sagani is screaming," Elzeth said.

"I would, too, if I was trapped with him all day."

Ghosthands stood and spread his arms out wide. To Tomas's dismay, it looked as though the rocking of the train didn't bother him in the least.

"It's not glorious because of the view. It's glorious

because this is the place where you finally die. The place you can lay your burdens down. It feels—fitting, doesn't it?"

Tomas didn't care for the conversation, so he drew his sword, the nexus ready. Ghosthands held up a hand. "One question before we begin."

Tomas waited. As long as Ghosthands was up here, he wasn't threatening Angela and Rachel.

"What form did Elzeth take when he found you?" Ghosthands asked.

That was about the last question Tomas expected, but he replied, "A mountain cat."

Then curiosity got the best of him. "What about you?"

"A snake. It emerged from the mud and offered me a chance at salvation, a chance to serve the Creator I shunned in my first life."

Tomas started. "Wait. You joined the church *after* becoming a host?"

Ghosthands took a couple of steps forward. "Is it so hard for you to understand? The gate is the universe's greatest teacher. It shows us what is true when all our illusions are stripped away. Tell me, as you were dying, what did you think about?"

"Mostly how I didn't want to die."

"Pathetic!" Ghosthands shouted. There was a flash of something, a twisting of his face that betrayed him. Tomas's first impression had been correct. This wasn't the same man he'd fought outside Chesterton. Madness pulled at him just as it pulled at Tomas.

Ghosthands stomped on the roof. "You were given a precious gift, a few minutes when you could see beyond the illusion, but you were so focused on your own pitiful life you missed it! When I lay dying in the grass, I saw the Creator. I glimpsed just the slightest shadow of His plan, and it was magnificent. I found my way to the Holy Father and shared with him my vision, and he welcomed me into the church with open arms. He gave me the purpose my previous excuse for a life had lacked."

"Even though your beliefs damn your soul?"

"It's not about me!" Ghosthands roared with a vehemence that startled Tomas back half a step.

"It was never about me. It's about Him and what I can do for His plan. My life doesn't matter. I died the day the demon visited me. The gate just hasn't stolen my soul yet."

Ghosthands's eyes blazed. "And besides, my soul isn't damned. The Creator waits for me. I know it to be true."

The assassin leaped forward, surprising Tomas. He'd halfway hoped Ghosthands would rant until an opening presented itself. Tomas retreated, suddenly wishing he had more space before he reached the end of the car.

As before, Ghosthands didn't waste any time testing Tomas. He attacked with incredible speed, made even more impressive by the terrible choice of the battlefield. Tomas allowed the power of the nexus to flow through him. He didn't lose track of Elzeth as he had before, but the moment of disorientation almost proved fatal.

Ghosthands backed Tomas up almost to the edge of the car before Tomas found his footing and countered. But Ghosthands didn't budge. Tomas wasn't fast enough to get inside his guard and, after a moment, was forced to retreat. His foot slipped off the car, and for a terrifying heartbeat, he thought he would fall between the cars and be run over by the train.

Instead, he fell backward, hit the back of his head, and collapsed in an awkward heap on the platform of the next car, the one Ghosthands had turned into a graveyard for the Army escort. Tomas scooted back and held his sword high, expecting Ghosthands to follow, but the church assassin remained on the first roof.

Tomas grumbled, rubbed the back of his head to see if he'd cut his skull, then stood up. "Not sure if we're going to pull this off without unity," he said.

"Not up for debate," Elzeth answered.

Tomas crossed over to the first passenger car, then looked through the window in the door. As near as he could tell, Rachel and Angela were holding up well. They were standing at the other end of the car, surrounded by the army escort with their rifles ready. The door behind them, which led to the engine, looked well barricaded.

It wasn't perfect, but it would do.

He grabbed hold of the ladder and climbed back to the roof. Ghosthands had returned to the center of the car and was waiting. Tomas shook out his arms, then advanced cautiously.

Their next exchange didn't end in Tomas's favor. The nexus gave him incredible strength and speed, but he never got close to cutting Ghosthands. He backed up, and Ghosthands didn't follow.

"What's wrong? You were stronger before," Ghosthands said.

Tomas ignored the question to talk to Elzeth. "I'm going to need everything you can give me."

He felt Elzeth's determination in his answer. The sagani might not risk unity, but he didn't want to die any more than Tomas. "Absolutely."

A fresh wave of strength filled Tomas's limbs, and he charged forward. Elzeth burned as bright as he ever had, and the nexus added fuel to the fire. The rocking of the car became easy to compensate for. Ghosthands moved slower than before. Tomas stood against Ghosthands's flashing steel and was pleased to see Ghosthands be the first to give ground. He pressed harder, seeking the one cut, the one opening that would give him a definitive advantage.

Ghosthands retreated another step and then another, but Tomas never gave him a chance to breathe. Their swords moved ever faster, and finally, Tomas found his gap. He snapped his wrists and cut at Ghosthands's exposed shoulder.

It should have been a strike that brought the fight to its end.

Except that was the moment the train slammed on its brakes, sending both Tomas and Ghosthands flying forward.

29

Tomas woke to the sounds of a storm. He cracked one eye open and saw a flash of light that he first thought was lightning. Like lightning, a boom of thunder followed the flash. But there was no rain.

Where was he?

His thoughts crawled in random directions, and he couldn't seem to corral them. He lay facedown in tall grass, and as his senses returned, pain washed over him. He pressed his hands into the dirt and pushed himself to his knees. His body groaned and creaked, but the pain was diffuse, leading him to believe he hadn't broken any bones or punctured any organs.

At least, he hoped he hadn't.

More lightning and thunder rolled across the plains, sending a sharp pain stabbing through his skull. He clutched at his head, but it did little to ease his suffering.

"Elzeth? You still there?"

Silence answered him, but he felt the sagani slumbering within. Dormant, but not gone.

Thoughts finally fell into place, one after the other. He'd

been fighting Ghosthands, and the train had stopped. He looked around.

The sudden stop had thrown him from the roof of the car. He'd landed and tried to roll, but had hit his head in the attempt and blacked out. The train still rested where it had stopped, a mighty machine slumbering in the middle of nowhere.

More lightning and thunder, and this time he saw it was coming from the first car.

Where Angela said that she would wait. Where she protected Rachel.

He stumbled toward the car, but it moved farther away. He squinted, realizing several moments too late that the train was moving again. Steam hissed and wheels clanked as it searched for the momentum of before. Tomas took two faltering steps toward it, and Elzeth suddenly flared to life. The sagani took in the situation much faster than Tomas.

"You're going to need a sword and that shard of nexus."

Tomas cursed and looked around. It wasn't hard to trace the path his body had created. Grass was broken and bent in a straight line, and he retreated along the line until he found his sword. He looked it over and was pleased to see it was unharmed. He apologized to the blade and returned it to its sheath.

Tomas spun in a circle, looking for the nexus. He couldn't see the distinctive blue glow anywhere. For a moment, he feared Ghosthands had found it first. If he had, that would be the end of their hope.

He spun again. The train was slowly picking up speed, and the rifles continued to fire. He didn't have time for this.

"Where's the nexus?"

"To your right," Elzeth said.

Tomas followed Elzeth's guidance, and sure enough, he

soon spotted the familiar glow. He picked the shard up and let the power of the nexus flow through him. It might destroy his body, but if he survived the day, he didn't care. He ran after the train, jumping onto the penultimate passenger car before it could pull away.

The rest of the passengers had collected near the rear of the train, crouching behind benches as though that would give them protection. They stared at him, but Tomas ignored them. He ran forward, jumping from one car to the next.

By the time he reached the first passenger car, the train was moving at full speed once again. Someone had kicked the door at the rear of the passenger car off its hinges, and Tomas poked his head around the frame.

What he first saw made no sense. The last of the army escort was dead, leaving only Angela and Rachel alive. The two women were standing about where Tomas had left them, but Angela had a knife to Rachel's throat and was hiding behind her.

They weren't alone. A man of average height stood in the middle of the car, arms out wide to appear non-threatening. The bloody knives he held in his hands ruined the effect, though. Tomas saw the chains attached to the blades and knew instantly that he was looking at an inquisitor.

Of course, Ghosthands wouldn't have boarded the train by himself. The church would have brought more support than a handful of knights.

So Angela had done the only thing that kept her and Rachel alive. The church needed Rachel's mind, and so the marshal and the inquisitor were at an impasse.

Angela's eyes widened slightly when she saw Tomas. It was an instinctive reaction, one she froze as soon as she realized it. But it was all the warning the inquisitor needed. He spun, the knives already flying.

Tomas was ready. He sprinted through the door as the first knife missed. The inquisitor yanked it back and started spinning, sending both knives for Tomas.

Had he stayed in the aisle, they would have posed more of a problem. But he leaped onto the back of the benches, running across them with precise steps. The approach caught the inquisitor by surprise. He shifted his angles, but he was too late. Tomas leaped at him, and the inquisitor pulled his knives in, but he was too slow. Elzeth wasn't burning that brightly, but the strength of the nexus more than made up for the lack.

Tomas cut down. The inquisitor's reactions kept him from death, but Tomas's sword still bit deep into his shoulder. The inquisitor's left arm went limp. Before Tomas could finish the task, though, the blade returned to the inquisitor's right hand. He cut at Tomas.

Still too slow, though.

Tomas stepped back and let the knife pass harmlessly in front of him, then reached out with his sword and stabbed the inquisitor through the heart. He pulled his sword out and took a step back. The inquisitor summoned the strength for one more attack, but he collapsed to the ground before he could cut Tomas. He died with a glare on his face.

Tomas was breathing hard, and the pain in his body remained. His head still felt like something was exploding within.

Something wasn't right.

He didn't know how long the fall had knocked him unconscious, but he had the feeling that it hadn't been long. Perhaps he wasn't healed as much as he thought.

But that didn't feel right. It was more than that. Elzeth

wasn't acting the way Tomas was used to. Then a fresh wave of pain crashed over him. He clutched at his stomach, not because he felt sick, but because it felt as though Elzeth was sick. His sword hand twitched, but Tomas forced it back to stillness.

Hells, he was a mess.

But the fight was over. At least for now. He didn't know what had happened to Ghosthands, but the train was moving, and he didn't think there were any threats left on board.

He turned to the two women. "I think we won."

The victory had cost them too much. Tomas teetered on the edge of madness, and the fight had wiped out an entire army unit. But they'd won. Tomas held onto that idea. Whatever the cost, victory made it worthwhile.

He couldn't read the expression on Rachel's face, but he imagined she was still in shock after all she'd seen. She was a scholar who'd spent her life in a lab. This was nothing like the life she'd known.

But there was no misinterpreting the relief on Angela's face. She sagged back, taking her knife away from Rachel's neck. She leaned back against the makeshift barricade and closed her eyes. "About damn time. Sorry about that, Rachel. It was the only thing I could think of in the moment."

Rachel nodded. Her voice was calm, considering everything she'd just been through. "I understand. We all do what we need to."

Tomas agreed. That, maybe, was as good a saying as he'd ever heard to describe his own life. He didn't have the plans people wanted him to have, but he'd always done all that he needed to, and maybe that was enough. He wiped the blood off his blade and sheathed it. Hopefully, he'd never have to draw it again.

He took what felt like the first deep breath in a long time.

A knife appeared, as if by magic, in Rachel's hand. Tomas blinked, not understanding.

Rachel spun the knife with practiced ease, reversing her grip on the blade.

Then she stabbed it deep into Angela's stomach.

30

F or a long moment, Tomas just stared. He saw the scene before him, painted in vivid detail. Angela's eyes had shot open wide and stared down at her stomach. Blood seeped from the wound and spread down Angela's shirt. Rachel smiled and pulled the knife out, twisting as she did.

Tomas had his sword back in his hand before the impact of what he was witnessing hit him. He raised it as he took a step toward the women, then froze when he heard the tread of boots on the floor behind him.

"Tomas!" Ghosthands called his name with malicious, twisted glee.

Tomas spun. He couldn't help Angela with Ghosthands ready to pounce. The sight froze him in place, and he wondered if he looked as broken as the church assassin. Ghosthands looked almost as though a herd of cows had trampled him. His flesh was mottled with bruises, his nose was twisted at an unnatural angle, and his face looked like someone had taken a rough-grit sandpaper to it. Despite the wounds, Ghosthands's eyes blazed with joy, and his smile stretched from ear to ear.

Ghosthands attacked, his laughter echoing through the car. Tomas pulled from the nexus and called on Elzeth's aid. Swords clashed and clashed again, Ghosthands so close Tomas could smell his sweat and feel the heat coming off his skin. The sagani within him must have been a raging inferno.

The benches crowded them on both sides, preventing either from moving effectively from side to side. The bodies of the soldiers clogged the aisle as well, making every step a gamble.

The complications didn't bother Ghosthands. His laughter didn't stop, and Tomas had no doubt that madness had the assassin's mind in a tight grip. Often, when Tomas had come across a host seized by madness, he'd had little to fear. Sagani burned brightest at the end of their lives, but that extra strength was usually offset by a lack of skill and coordination.

Ghosthands enjoyed all the advantages of madness while suffering from none of the weaknesses. His cuts were stronger and faster than Tomas had ever seen them, but they were as precise and as controlled as any master swordsman.

There was a moment, as Tomas gave up ground to the assassin, that he wondered if he was wrong. Maybe this wasn't madness but an evolution of what it meant to be a host. Maybe Ghosthands had found a new level—a mountain peak Tomas hadn't learned how to climb.

It wasn't beyond reason. Ulva had hinted at a different way forward, as had Ghosthands outside of Chesterton.

Whether madness or mastery, Tomas knew one truth deep in his heart. He wasn't strong enough to win. He searched for an opening, but anytime he lashed out, Ghosthands was already there. Where his own defense was concerned, he always blocked a moment too late. Ghosthands hadn't made the fatal cut yet, but a dozen shallow ones proved almost as damning.

Tomas risked a leap backward. His left foot landed solidly, but his right rolled on the arm of a corpse. It took him a moment to regain his balance, and Ghosthands pressed the attack.

Tomas scrambled up onto a bench, then retreated along the backs as Ghosthands cheerfully cut at his knees and ankles. Tomas hated retreating away from Angela, but the lack of space took too many options away. When Ghosthands gave him a moment to breathe, he jumped back to the aisle, this time able to spot his landing.

Ghosthands pressed hard, but Tomas had better footing here, and for a moment, the duel was on the verge of tipping in his favor.

Inside Tomas, Elzeth screamed, a primal mix of frustration, fear, and anger. The sagani burned even brighter, and Tomas feared Elzeth would burn so brightly they would have no choice but to unify. The sagani stopped just short, leaving the barest shred of a veil standing between them.

The additional strength surged through Tomas, and he pushed hard, knowing he would never have a better chance. He cut and stabbed, trying every trick he knew to gain an advantage.

Ghosthands stood up to the assault. His own offensive had halted against the onslaught, but Tomas simply couldn't get to the assassin. Every opening closed a moment before Tomas reached it. The difference between them wasn't much more than the width of a hair, but it was a chasm Tomas couldn't cross on his own.

The answer was obvious.

He knew the only way to kill Ghosthands and save Angela was to unify. His blood ran cold at the thought, but as Rachel had said, some things just needed to be done.

His heart hammered at the thought. Unity didn't mean death. Just... disappearance. An end to what he was.

But this was what the situation demanded. It didn't have to be any harder than that.

He briefly tried burning the last shred of separation between him and Elzeth, but he couldn't do that to Elzeth. This was a mutual suicide of souls. He didn't even know if the gate would open for him when his body gave out. It would destroy Elzeth, too.

Tomas retreated another step, and he put the question to Elzeth. The sagani could read the situation just as well as he could. In unity, they might just be strong enough. "Do we do it?"

The sagani stayed firmly silent, but his disapproval came strongly through their bond. It shouted "No," even as Elzeth refused to answer out loud.

Tomas tried to burn the veil on his own, but he felt Elzeth cool rapidly, solidifying their separation. The sagani kept his promise, dooming them both.

Tomas could force the issue. It was still his body, and if he acted fast enough, he thought he could forcibly unify them.

It was a betrayal of the worst kind, though, and he didn't crave unity strongly enough to summon the will.

So that was that. If they were going to win this fight, they had to do it without unity. Elzeth burned brighter as Tomas backed away, bringing them again right to the edge of unity, and Tomas summoned the last of his own strength and energy.

He cut Ghosthands close to the shoulder. It wasn't much

more than a scratch, but triumph surged in Tomas's breast. They could do it!

Ghosthands's blade disappeared, and Tomas realized too late that he'd been fooling himself this entire time.

They had never been as close as Tomas thought. Ghosthands sliced through Tomas's defenses, opening up new wounds across his arms and torso. Tomas had no choice but to retreat, leaving Angela even further behind.

Unity offered the only hope. One he had to grasp alone.

He took a step back, summoning the will to end both him and Elzeth.

He couldn't.

Unity waited, but his will was insufficient. He didn't want it enough.

Instead, he summoned the last of his strength, seeking that one deadly cut. He focused all his strength into one last series of attacks, but it was all for naught. Ghosthands shredded him when he got close, and the exchange ended with Tomas staggering back under half a dozen fresh wounds.

Ghosthands grinned even wider, ripping open some of the freshly healed scabs on his face. He smiled like a politician who'd just won a coveted election. He strode forward, and Tomas couldn't follow the speed of the blade. One step of retreat became a second and then a third. Distance couldn't save him, though, and he suffered deeper cuts as Ghosthands pushed him out onto the platform of the train.

Tomas tried one last time to land a killing blow, but he was at his limit. He looked around for something in the environment that he could use, but there was nothing nearby. The platform was empty except for the two warriors.

He snarled, unable to express his hate in words alone, but Ghosthands's smile only grew wider.

"Goodbye, Tomas," the assassin said.

And with that, he kicked out, catching Tomas straight in the chest. Tomas flew backward. The railing of the platform caught the back of his legs, and for a moment, Tomas thought he might save his balance.

But the force of the kick was too great. He tipped over backward. He reached out for the railing, hoping to grasp any handhold.

But he was too slow. Elzeth strengthened his body one last time as he went cartwheeling off the platform, and he was thrown off a moving train for the second time that day.

Tomas hit the ground hard and let go of his sword, afraid he would stab himself as he fell. He tumbled end over end, only Elzeth's strength preventing him from breaking bones. But by the time he came to a stop, the last car of the train was well past him.

Tomas stumbled to his feet, tried to take a step forward, and fell.

Elzeth, again, flickered into silence, and Tomas didn't think he would rouse the sagani soon. Elzeth was exhausted, too.

All he could do was crawl on hands and knees as the train chugged away.

31

Quinton's fight against Tomas was nothing compared to the fight that now raged for control of his body. The demon inside him fought far harder than it ever had. For years it had been caged and tightly controlled, but madness widened the bars of its cage and gave it hope. It even fought harder than it had when it and Quinton had first joined on the bank of the river. Then, it hadn't understood the control Quinton would exert over it.

Now it did, and it fought like the demon it was for a taste of freedom.

There could only be one victor, though, just like him and Tomas.

After their first battle in Porum, Quinton feared that Tomas had somehow gained the upper hand. He'd been so strong. But Tomas on the train had barely been a challenge. He'd spent more time considering the best punishment for Tomas than he did thinking about how to beat the rebellious host.

Quinton had considered killing Tomas before realizing

that leaving him to die of madness was the worst punishment he could devise.

He'd beaten Tomas, and he'd be damned if he let the demon beat him now.

Bit by bit, Quinton wrestled the demon back into its cage and tightened its bars. When he was back in firm control, he returned to the car. Rachel stood among the bodies of the soldiers, calmly wiping the blood from her knife. Angela was propped up against the barricade, clutching her wound.

"Did they hurt you?" Quinton asked.

Rachel scoffed. "I told them I was on the run from the church. They thought they had to protect me."

Quinton blinked. His path rarely intersected with that of the church scholars, but even he knew of Rachel by reputation. She had sent more hosts to the gates in her experiments than he had with his sword. It was said that her heart was colder than ice.

"Regardless, I am glad to see you well. Your loss would set our efforts back by years, if not decades."

"Thank you for your assistance," she said, but Quinton noticed the gleam in her eye. "Does Father know you are succumbing to madness?"

If she'd hoped to get a rise from him, she was disappointed. "He does not, but once we've safely gotten you west, I plan to tell him. I hope he will allow me to end my life."

Now her disappointment showed. "I would study you, if I could."

"I will help as I am able, but nothing will stop me from dying by my own hand."

She gave him a slight bow, then pointed to Angela. "What should we do about her?"

Quinton looked her over. Rachel's stab was fatal, but it

would be a while before Angela died. It would be a slow and painful death. Killing her quickly would be a mercy. He almost drew his sword to finish what Rachel had started. Angela was a demon-lover, but Quinton forgave her for her sins, just as the Creator would.

A better idea soon occurred to him, though. Why waste a death? Here, she'd just be another casualty among many. But she could serve as a punishment for one who deserved to rot in each of the three hells.

He picked Angela up and walked her out to the platform. She struggled, but an angry child would have put up more of a fuss. Rachel followed, curious.

Without fanfare, Quinton threw Angela off the same side of the train he'd kicked Tomas. He didn't know if Tomas would attempt to pursue the train on foot, but he suspected the fool would try. If he did, he'd be rewarded with the corpse of another woman important to him. Quinton had killed Narkissa, and now he'd killed Angela.

He breathed in deeply, smiling as Angela's body twisted and tumbled to a stop by the side of the tracks.

His revenge was complete, and he believed he could die content.

Tomas ran after the train, staying close to the tracks. It was already miles ahead of him and gaining distance fast, but what else could he do? Angela was on that train, and he'd promised he'd keep her safe.

He kept calling for Elzeth, but his shouting did nothing to wake the sagani. He had only his own muscles and conditioning to rely on, and they weren't sufficient.

Ghosthands had beaten him, but he wasn't dead yet. There had to be something more he could do.

He lost track of time. All that mattered was putting one foot in front of the other. The train was barely visible near the edge of the horizon and would soon be out of sight, and he tried to use that knowledge to push himself harder. But his body had already been through too much, and there was only so much left to give.

One foot in front of the other. He wouldn't give up.

His sense of failure chased him and pushed him harder. If he had only united with Elzeth, they might have had a chance. But when the moment had come, he'd turned coward and run. He'd finally faced his most fearsome opponent, and it was himself.

One foot in front of the other.

He didn't know how many miles had passed when Elzeth stirred. The sagani rumbled but was more of a smoldering ember than a burning fire. "Glad to have you back, old friend."

Elzeth didn't answer, but Tomas felt the sentiment returned. Then, a sense of alarm passed through their connection.

"What is it?" Tomas asked.

"I smell something. Blood."

Tomas slowed to a stop. The world twisted, and he put his hands on his knees to stabilize himself. Once a bit of awareness returned, Tomas smelled it, too. He raised his nose and sniffed, then followed the scent.

When he saw the source, he let out a strangled cry.

"Oh, Tomas," Elzeth said. The sagani's grief mirrored Tomas's own, an endless expanse of sorrow Tomas would never cross, no matter how much longer he lived.

Tomas ran forward and fell down next to Angela's body.

Several of her limbs were at unnatural angles, and the blood had spread almost all the way across her shirt.

Somehow, she was still breathing, but Tomas didn't need to be a healer to know the truth. He looked around, but they were in the middle of nowhere, dozens of miles from help.

He grabbed her right hand, which remained limp in his grip. He brought his lips to the back of her hand and kissed it, his tears falling on the grass next to her body.

"I'm sorry," he sobbed. "I'm so, so, sorry."

She didn't answer.

Tomas feared he'd never hear her voice again.

He sat down next to her, held her hand in his own, and began her death vigil.

"Promise me one thing," he told Elzeth.

"Name it."

"Before we die, we're going to kill that man."

Elzeth burned brightly, comforting Tomas as the storm he'd just outrun earlier that day closed on him. The sagani spoke, solemn as Tomas had ever heard him.

"I promise that before we die, we're going to kill that man."

ABOUT THE AUTHOR

Ryan Kirk is the bestselling author of the *Nightblade* series of books. When he isn't writing, you can probably find him playing disc golf or hiking through the woods.

RyanKirkAuthor.com
contact@waterstonemedia.net

 facebook.com/waterstonemedia

twitter.com/waterstonebooks

instagram.com/waterstonebooks

Milton Keynes UK
Ingram Content Group UK Ltd.
UKHW021628030823
426258UK00011B/74